The PARENT TRAP

Adaptation by VIC CRUME

Based on the screenplay and written for the screen by David Swift

SCHOLASTIC BOOK SERVICES

NEW YORK · TORONTO · LONDON · AUCKLAND · SYDNEY · TOKYO

The characters in this book were played in the motion picture *The Parent Trap* by:

Sharon McKendrick	Hayley Mills
Susan Evers	Hayley Mills
Margaret (Maggie) McKendrick	Maureen O'Hara
Mitch Evers	Brian Keith
Charles McKendrick	Charlie Ruggles
Verbena	Una Merkel
Reverend Dr. Moseby	Leo G. Carroll
Vicky Robinson	Joanna Barnes
Louise McKendrick	Cathleen Nesbitt
Miss Inch	Ruth McDevitt
Hecky	Crahan Denton
Edna Robinson	Linda Watkins
Miss Grunecker	Nancy Kulp
Chief Eaglewood	Frank DeVol

Written for the Screen and
Directed by David Swift
Based on a book by Erich Kästner

ISBN: 0-590-02961-4

23 22 21 20 19 18 17   2 3 4/8

CONTENTS

Spit and Image   5

Arapahoe Clobber   11

Revenge   16

Cabin Mates   24

The Plan   30

18 Belgrave Square   38

The Ranch   46

Warning   53

Shocking News   64

Strange Homecoming   71

Martinelli's-on-the-Terrace   81

Vicky Goes Camping   87

All Is Lost; Or Is It?   97

"For Now . . . For Always"   105

We call this one "Planning Stage — Camp Inch"

Spit and Image

SHARON McKENDRICK splashed her foot in the sparkling water of Lake Nakimquam. "You know," she said to the new friends and cabinmates who sat beside her on the small dock, "I think Camp Inch is great!"

Ursula and Betsy groaned. "That's because you haven't been coming here for four years," Betsy said. "My gosh! I know every single thing Miss Inch is going to say next!"

Ursula made her voice high and squeaky. "Now, campers! Your attention, please. Watch those demerits!"

Sharon giggled. "Is that supposed to be Miss Inch?" she asked.

"Just wait. You'll find out!" Ursula replied.

A short distance from the dock Miss Grunecker, the

5

camp athletic director, blew her whistle. She towered over the smallest campers lined up for cradle-class swim instruction. Out on the lake, campers dived off the float and splashed noisily about. Beyond them, campers in brightly painted canoes glided on the smooth blue surface of Lake Nakimquam.

"Hey! Look who's coming!" Ursula exclaimed.

Betsy squinted into the sunlight. "Hmm! Trouble!"

"Trouble? Who's trouble?" Sharon asked, looking out over the lake.

"Sue Trouble Evers, that's who!" Betsy replied. "You know — the girl we said you look like."

"Oh! *That* one!" Sharon shrugged. "Who are the other two?"

"Gwen and Cluny. They're all in Iroquois cabin. Last summer they beat us for Best Cabin Award, but we'll get 'em this year!"

Sharon laughed. "You know my grandmother kept saying, 'Now be sure your *tent* is well-ventilated.' My gosh! If she could see all the screens in Arapahoe *cabin*, she'd probably be thrilled!"

"Anyhow," Betsy said, "you do look alike."

Sharon giggled. "How do you know? You've never seen my grandmother."

"Oh, Sharon! You know what I mean! You and Susan. And *you've* noticed it too! *Both* of you noticed it. I saw you staring at each other yesterday when we were at the milk counter."

Ursula nodded. "And it isn't just having blue eyes and honey-blonde hair, either. It's when you have swim caps on that it *really* shows. Exactly the same features.

6

Why, I think you're practically identical!" She added quickly, "Of course, I don't mean the way you *act*."

Sharon scowled. "I *hope* not! She's chewing gum practically every second, and she bites her fingernails. And she's so loud! You can hear her all over the place!"

"Nevertheless," Betsy kicked at the water. Drops flew. "Nevertheless," she repeated. "I, for one, regard this as the beginning of the Famous Camp Inch Mystery. You're as alike as — as — "

Ursula nudged her. "Hey," she muttered. "Here they come!"

"Hi, Arapahoes!" Gwen called out.

The bow of the yellow canoe slid silently up within turning range of the dock. The Arapahoes watched the Iroquois' expert paddling. Susan reached out a deeply

tanned arm. She caught at the edge of the dock to keep the canoe from scraping as it slid up alongside. Her eyes met Sharon's. "What are you staring at?" she demanded.

Sharon flushed beneath her sunburn. "Excuse me. It's just that the girls were saying we look alike."

"Yeah? Turn your head. Let me see that profile!" Sue demanded. Sharon looked to the right.

Susan whooped! She slapped her knee. "I knew it! The spit and image of you-know-who!"

"Who?" all three Arapahoes chorused.

"Frankenstein!" Susan shouted. The Iroquois doubled over, laughing.

Loyal and angry Arapahoes acted. Out shot Ursula's foot. *Thud!* Betsy added another shove. In a split second, the Iroquois were dumped into the shallow water and the yellow canoe bobbed bottomside-up.

Susan, Gwen, and Cluny sputtered and staggered to the dock. Susan made a lunge for the nearest Arapahoe leg. Sharon scrambled out of reach as Ursula and Betsy, shrieking with laughter, danced back along the dock.

Susan shook both fists at them. "O.K., Arapahoes, O.K. But just watch out!"

At dinnertime, the Arapahoes — Sharon, Ursula, and Betsy — were already at their table in the big log-built dining hall when the three Iroquois walked in. Susan's nose was high in the air as she passed. Her fellow Iroquois, Gwen and Cluny, tilted theirs.

Betsy's hand smacked the table. "Well! Did you see that? The Three Little Pigs! Didn't they look snouty! I mean *snooty!*"

Ursula and Sharon rocked with giggles. "Oh! Betsy!" Sharon gasped. "You're terrible!"

Betsy looked across the dining hall. "Hey, do you see what I see? Look who's sitting by Miss Inch!"

The girls craned their necks to get a better view of the counselors' table. They could see Miss Grunecker chatting with a gray-haired man of about her age. He wore a khaki shirt with an orange scarf tucked inside the open collar.

"My goodness!" Sharon said. "Isn't he a little old for a Boy Scout?"

"Not him, silly!" Betsy exclaimed. "I mean the cute boy on the other side of Miss Inch."

Just then Miss Inch stood up. She rapped her glass with a teaspoon. "Attention, young ladies!" her voice shrilled through the dining room. "Your attention, girls!"

Ursula whispered, "Didn't I tell you?"

The voices and the rattling of plates in the dining hall died away. Miss Inch picked up a sheaf of white papers and began to read aloud: "Girls — old campers and new arrivals — welcome to Camp Inch on our first full day of the new camping season. I am — " she broke off and shuffled her papers — "oh, yes, here we are — I am — er — Miss Inch."

"Good thing she had her name written down," Betsy murmured. Sharon and Ursula — and others — shook with mirth. Miss Inch read on.

"At this time, I wish to introduce a visitor from the next hilltop over." Miss Inch waved her plump arm toward the left wall. "He is from the Thunderhead Boys Camp. Girls, meet Chief Eaglewood!"

9

The Camp Inchers clapped politely. Chief Eagle-wood rose and bowed. He spoke a few words, smiled, bowed again, then sat down.

Miss Inch beamed. "And now, girls, I have a little surprise for you. We're going to have a dance this coming Saturday night! And we've invited the Thunder-head Boys Camp to come over for this happy occasion!"

She was interrupted by wild squeals and clapping. She raised her hand. "Girls! Girls! Quiet, please. Trooper Stafford will now speak to us." She turned to the boy at her side. "Trooper Stafford, girls."

Trooper Stafford stood up. He spoke two words: "We accept," and sat down.

Susan Evers' loud whisper carried across the tables. "Oh! He's *darling!*"

Miss Inch waved her arms. "Just a word of warning, girls. Watch those demerits. Untidy little girls won't go to the dance. So keep those cabins clean, those uniforms spanking fresh, and we'll all be one big, happy family."

The Arapahoes glanced quickly toward the Iroquois' table. Susan was making a face and rolling her eyes toward the ceiling. "She's really awful!" Sharon thought.

The dinner hour ended.

Arapahoe Clobber

Moonlight shone with a ghostly light through the dark pines. Off the path, in the deepest shadows, three pajama-clad figures huddled near the door of Arapahoe cabin.

"Now, listen!" Sue hissed. "Let's get it straight. I go in first with the twine. Cluny, you plaster the place with honey. Really glop it on! Gwen, you do the same with the chocolate, then we'll all rig the booby trap and throw straw. Got it?"

They nodded.

"Come on, then. No noise!" Sue led the way.

There was enough light to see the three motionless figures lying on the cots. She opened the door. "Quick!" Gwen and Cluny slipped in. Each girl sped to work.

Up — Down — Across! Sue strung a spider's web of

twine over the sleepers. Cluny tilted a big jar of honey. It streamed out in folds of stickiness on blankets, pillowcases, and on the floor. Gwen carefully tipped a can of chocolate syrup over sneakers, shorts pockets, and into bathrobes. The hardest part was the booby trap — a pail filled with icy water. Working together, they slung it overhead. The slightest jar, and one of the luckless Arapahoes would have a pail of water on her head in the morning! Then came the straw. Everywhere it touched on honey, a gooey, bristly trail formed.

Work done, the Iroquois crept out into the dark woods.

"Boy, will they ever get demerits!" Gwen giggled.

"They won't be dancing with the Thunderhead boys. That's for sure!" Cluny whispered. They tried to choke back their laughter.

"Stop it!" Susan said sternly. "Do you want to wake the neighbors?"

All three Iroquois doubled over laughing. They went lurching down the dark path, out of sight.

Miss Inch breathed the pine air deep into her ample chest. She loved Saturday mornings — inspection day at Camp Inch. She turned to Miss Grunecker, who always went along on these occasions. "I believe we'll start inspection with Arapahoe cabin," she said.

"Very good choice. Very good," Miss Grunecker replied in her hearty voice. "Always start with the A's. Ho! Ho!" She laughed deeply.

Together, they started along the sandy path to the cabins. Miss Inch came to a sudden stop. She looked down. "Miss Grunecker! Am I mistaken, or is that hay I see?"

Miss Grunecker bent down. "It appears to be straw, Miss Inch," she reported.

"Straw! How strange!"

"Very strange. Very strange, indeed!" Miss Grunecker agreed.

Oddly enough, the trail of straw led straight to their goal — Arapahoe cabin!

"Oh, my gosh!" Betsy groaned. "Here they come! We're sunk!"

"Clobbered!" Betsy exclaimed.

"But can't we explain?" Sharon asked.

Ursula and Betsy shook their heads. "Isn't done," Betsy said, briefly.

Sharon flushed. "I didn't mean *tell*. I meant, couldn't we say it was an accident?"

Ursula shrugged. "Accident? Like how?"

Sharon drooped. "Oh," she said flatly. "I guess we couldn't."

Miss Inch and Miss Grunecker drew near the screened door. Miss Grunecker stepped ahead and rapped smartly. "Inspec-shun!" She opened the door for the Camp Directress.

"Horrors!" Miss Inch shrieked. She took one step forward and skidded dangerously in a pool of honey. Miss Grunecker dashed to the rescue, only to skid straight into Miss Inch's tottering form. They clung together for support.

In the silence that followed, three miserable Arapahoes faced the plump directress and the towering ath-

letic instructor. Betsy, chocolate-smeared, clutched a
stained bathrobe in her arms. From its upside down
pocket drops of chocolate syrup dripped with a steady
plop-plop-plop on the floor. Ursula seemed to be looped
in yards of twine. Honey and hay clung to her knees
and ankles. There was even a bristly patch of it on her
forehead. But it was Sharon who looked the most sensational! Her pale blue pajamas clung to her in soaking
wet ridges and folds. Her long blonde hair hung like
seaweed down to her shoulders; it was plastered in
snaky strands across her face. Her bare feet seemed to
have become small haystacks. Straw stuck out in all
directions.

Miss Inch's voice quivered. *"What is the meaning of
this?"*

"We were just cleaning up, Miss Inch," said Betsy, in
a small voice.

"Cleaning up! Cleaning UP!" Miss Inch's voice
choked with rage. "Well I should *think* so!" She glared.
"Whatever explanation there may be for this — this
mess — will wait. But there will be no dancing for Arapahoe campers tonight. You may be certain of that!"
She looked hard at each girl. "You may dance around
here with a scrub brush and mop. Immediately. That
is all!"

Angrily she turned to stride out the door. Her sneakers stuck in the honey. Miss Grunecker gave a helpful
tug. Together, they clopped out the door. Safe on the
sandy path once more, Miss Inch turned. "No dance!"
she snapped.

"Certainly *not!*" chimed in Miss Grunecker.

Through the screening, silent Arapahoes watched the pair. Miss Inch lifted each honey-and-hay-coated sneaker high off the ground at every step.

Suddenly, Sharon clapped a hand over her mouth. She shook with laughter.

"What's so funny?" Ursula asked, grimly.

Sharon rocked back and forth. "Miss Inch!" she finally gasped. "I saw that kind of walk once in a movie. Grandfather called it goosestepping!"

Revenge

BUT NO ARAPAHOE was laughing that night. The trio stood below the porch railing looking up at the bright scene beyond the screened windows of Recreation Hall. Fellow campers dipped, twirled, bobbed, and turned to the music of the record player.

"I'm so mad I could spit!" Betsy snapped.

"That Susan Evers! What a rotten trick!" Ursula said — as she had been saying all day.

"Look!" Sharon cried.

Susan Evers, in palest lavender-pink, bounced into view with her partner.

"Trooper Stafford!" Betsy breathed. "Wouldn't you know she'd get him!"

The music stopped. Susan and her partner moved away from the window. The porch doors opened.

"Duck!" Betsy hissed. She pulled at Ursula's and Sharon's elbows. "They're coming out here!"

"Get under the porch!" Betsy whispered.

Overhead footsteps thumped straight for the porch railing. The Arapahoes carefully edged out from their hiding place and looked up. Sue half-sat, half-leaned on the railing. Her lavender-pink skirt swung temptingly just over their heads. Ursula nudged Sharon. "Wait! I'll be back. Got an idea." Moving silently, she crept to the porch corner, then scooted out.

Above them Susan's voice could be plainly heard. "Oh, camp's O.K., I guess. I'm not coming back to this one though. It's so juvenile. They treat you like a baby."

There was a pause. Trooper Stafford changed the subject. "Where are you from?" he asked.

"Carmel. Carmel-by-the-Sea. That's in California. Actually, our ranch is in Monterey County."

"That's great!"

Susan said, "Oh, you'd love California. At least I do. It's so sort of . . . I don't know, marvelous, actually."

"It sounds great." Trooper Stafford replied.

"Great conversation." Betsy whispered to Sharon.

Betsy and Sharon were so interested in what would be said next that they didn't hear Ursula coming back. Sharon almost gave away their hiding place by yelling, when her arm was suddenly pressed by Ursula's fingers.

"Ssh!" Ursula whispered. "Look!"

In her hand was a pair of scissors. She motioned Sharon and Betsy to follow her.

"Oh, it's absolute fun living in California," Susan

was saying as the Arapahoes emerged from under the porch. "Every year when I get back from camp Dad takes me on a trek into the mountains."

Trooper Stafford sounded surprised. "You mean your mother lets you just go up in the mountains like that?"

"Oh, I don't have a mother. Just Dad and me. And of course, Hecky." Susan replied. "He's our ranch foreman. He's wonderful. He tells sensational stories."

"Like what?" asked Trooper Stafford, interestedly.

Ursula carefully reached up. Being careful not to pull at Susan's skirt, she swiftly cut upward from the hem to as high as she could reach. She handed the scissors to Sharon.

Susan's voice went on without a pause. "Oh, Hecky used to be a rodeo rider. He can tell you more exciting things! You know — bulldogging, and roping, and bronc bustin' — things like that."

Sharon handed the scissors to Betsy. "Careful!" she whispered.

Betsy stood up. She held her breath. She had the hardest job — connecting the cuts made by Ursula and Sharon. She would have to cut straight across to take out a panel. She was on the last snip when the music began.

Susan said, "Oh, they've started the music again."

"Guess we ought to go in, huh?"

"Oh, yes. I just love dancing. I could just dance all night — especially with you, Wilfred."

The two moved away from the railing toward the door. In back of them the Arapahoes waited and watched — to see Sue's white cotton briefs make their sensational public appearance before all of Camp Inch and its guests.

Sharon waved the cut-out piece of skirt. "Oh boy! Any minute now!" They ducked down.

There was a flurry of footsteps on the porch. Cluny's voice was angry. "But where *were* you? Where could she have done it?"

"I wasn't anywhere. I just went out, and . . ."

The Arapahoes popped up and stepped out to the porch pathway. "Serves you right," Sharon called out, grinning. "Stay out of our cabin from now on."

Susan sprang forward. "You vicious little wretch!" she screamed. In a flash, Sharon was up the steps. Sue swung her hand and slapped her look-alike squarely across the face.

Sharon heaved Susan backward and landed her own stinging slap. Gwen and Cluny, Ursula and Betsy, leaped to the rescue. "Sharon! Susan! Quit it!" But the fight was on. Slapping and pushing, the girls edged each other to the door of Recreation Hall.

As campers inside heard the commotion they started for the porch, only to be knocked back inside as Susan and Sharon tumbled in. Someone's foot caught the leg of the table, and over went the record player and a stack of records. In the heaving, lurching excitement, the refreshment table was the next to go. It tilted on end like a seesaw, and cakes slid gracefully along its sloping length. Miss Grunecker grabbed at one, Miss Inch seized another. As Chief Eaglewood came rushing past to separate the fighting girls, a huge punch

bowl, moving at the same speed, came skimming down the tilted table, and the two moving bodies collided. Chief Eaglewood was awash with sticky punch, and decorated with circles of lemon slices that only a moment before had been floating gently in the punch bowl.

Betsy heard Miss Inch's voice right next to her. "I've got a cake in my hands. Now *stop it!*"

Betsy turned — and saw an unbelievable sight! Miss Inch had lifted the cake plate high over her head, and unknowingly had plunged it right into the carved beak of a totem-pole bird. Miss Inch lowered the plate — there was no cake on it! A strange dazed look came over her face. Mystified, she looked up. Plunk! Down came the cake, and Miss Inch became a kind of weird dessert as her features disappeared beneath a mound of pale pink strawberry icing. Her shriek was muffled: "You little *wretches!*"

It was too much! Betsy fled.

Morning sun streamed across Miss Inch's desk. Miss Grunecker went to the window of the camp office and tilted up the Venetian blinds. Miss Inch sat back in her chair. She stared coldly at the two campers standing before her desk.

Sharon shifted her weight from one foot to the other. "I wonder if she'll send me home?" she thought uneasily.

In the dead silence of Miss Inch's office, Susan suddenly snapped her chewing gum.

At the sound, Sharon stiffened. "Even if I'm sent home," she told herself, "it was worth it!"

Miss Inch leaned forward. Miss Grunecker, looking taller than ever, stood by, arms folded. Miss Inch pressed both plump hands flat on the desk. "Well, congratulations, girls. In the history of our camp yours was the most infamous, most revolting, most disgusting display of hooliganism we have ever had!"

"*Ever* had!" Miss Grunecker said helpfully. "Brawling like hooligans!" "Worst of all," Miss Inch continued, "two sisters, who should be setting a good example."

"Oh, no!" said Miss Grunecker. "Not sisters, Miss Inch. Just look-alikes."

"I've never seen her before in my life!" Sharon said

scornfully. Susan's blue eyes blazed. "I guess I've been lucky!" she snapped back. Miss Inch held out an ash tray. "You may deposit your gum, Sharon." "I'm *Susan!*" Susan said indignantly.

"Amazing resemblance!" Miss Inch shook her head. "I gather that you girls don't get along together?"

Susan and Sharon exchanged brief but unfriendly looks.

"Well, as the composers Gilbert and Sullivan wrote — let the punishment fit the crime. You will return to your cabins, pack your luggage, and await Miss Grunecker and myself."

Sharon hesitated. "Should we wait in our traveling clothes?" she asked.

"Certainly not!" said Miss Inch. "There are four weeks left of camp, and you'll spend them all together. As I said, the punishment will fit the crime. You'll room together, eat together, play together. Either you'll find a way to live with each other or you'll spend the time punishing yourselves far better than I ever could. That is all, girls."

Cabin Mates

AN HOUR LATER the two had moved their luggage and were settled in the cabin they were to share together for better or worse.

"Four more weeks of this!" Sharon thought disgustedly. She dug her elbows into the mattress and pretended to read her poetry book.

Susan, her back turned, bent over her own cot. She arranged photographs and snapshots on the blanket, switching them from place to place.

"I'll never forgive that Gwen and Cluny," she thought, angrily. "Marching along with all the other kids just as though they thought they were in a parade! Why, they acted as though it was a big joke, me getting stuck with that Sharon McKendrick! Everybody in camp followed us here!" Susan picked up a photograph and thumbtacked it to the wall. A sudden puff of breeze stirred the pictures on the cot. "Oh, darn!" She bent to straighten them. Then a gust of wind blew in, pushing raindrops before it. The pictures sailed into the air. "Oh!" Susan shrieked. "Oh!"

Sharon sprang off her cot. "Oh, my goodness! Hurry! Quick!" She ran to the screening and tried to lower the canvas curtain. It flapped and billowed in the increasing wind. Rain came flying into the cabin. "Help, Susan!" Sharon called.

Together, the girls managed to fasten the canvas tight. They turned to look at the room. Snapshots and photographs, splotched with rain, lay everywhere on the floor. "Oh, gosh, look at this mess!" Sue bent to pick up pictures, one by one.

Sharon dropped to her knees and gathered up all of those within arm's reach. "Are they ruined?" she asked, doubtfully.

Susan stood up. "Well, it didn't do them any good. Look at this one." She held out a large photograph. It was covered with star-shaped rain puckers.

"Oh, that's a shame! Who is he?"

Susan stared. "Are you kidding? Ricky Nelson."

"Oh, is he your boy friend?"

An astonished look came over Susan's face. "Say, Sharon — are you from outer space?"

"Oh, no!" Sharon quickly replied. "I'm from Boston."

Susan's eyes widened. "Oh!" she said, quickly. She abruptly turned to face the wall. "Imagine not knowing a big entertainer like Ricky Nelson!" she thought.

Sharon was certainly a queer one. But Sue smiled to herself as she waited for the dinner bell to ring.

An hour later, the screened door banged. Sharon looked up from the small table where she was working. She stood the little traveling iron up on end.

"Hey, what are you doing?" Susan asked, walking over to the table. "My pictures! Sharon! What a *wonderful* idea!"

Sharon smiled. "Well, I just got to thinking — maybe they'd iron out." She paused. "I was very careful. I tested it on one of my own first."

"Great!" Susan picked up a large photograph Sharon had placed on the cot. "This is my dad. Dreamy. Yes?"

"He's very handsome," Sharon answered. "It must be fun — those trips up in the mountains." She flushed, remembering how she had learned about them.

Susan looked puzzled. Then her face cleared. She laughed. "You were under the porch! Well, you're right. It's great. Ever been to California?"

Sharon shook her head.

"Well, it's a sensational place. At least, our ranch is. It's out in Carmel near the ocean. I've got a horse and everything. And we have a pool. You know, you can practically fall out the front door and go swimming any time you like."

Sharon put down the iron. She flung herself on her cot. Susan stacked the dry snapshots. "Susan," Sharon began, then hesitated. "Why have you been coming to Camp Inch for four years? I mean — well, with a horse and a ranch and everything," she stumbled. "Well, what I mean is — going up in the mountains with your dad

26

— well, I just wouldn't want to come all the way from California to Maine just for Camp Inch. Not if I had a father like yours!" Her face turned pink.

Susan flopped across her cot. "Have a Fig Newton," she said, holding out a box of cookies.

Sharon took a convenient handful. "Thanks." She kept her eyes on the cookies. "I'm sorry, Susan. It isn't any of my business. It's just that — well, if I had a father like that, wild horses couldn't drag me away!"

Susan rolled over on her stomach. "Why? Is your father the busy type?"

"I don't have a father. That is — actually, Mother and Daddy separated years ago. I never saw him. Not to remember him, anyhow."

There was a short silence. Then Susan spoke. She cleared her throat. "Well, as a matter of fact, I don't have a mother." She glanced toward Sharon. "I guess that's why Daddy sends me to Camp Inch. He figures Miss Inch is the next best thing, maybe." She twisted over on her side. "You know, it's scary the way nobody stays together anymore these days. Pretty soon it's going to be more divorces than marriages."

Sharon sighed. "Isn't that the truth!"

"How old are you?" Susan asked.

"Thirteen."

"So am I. When will you be fourteen?"

"November twelfth."

Susan sat up. "You will! That's my birthday too."

Sharon stared. She balanced the last Fig Newton on her knee. "That's funny!"

"Yeah!" Susan stared back.

Sharon arose and walked to the screened door.

"Stopped raining," she announced. "Want to go down and get a popsicle, or something?"

Sue didn't move. "Sharon, you said you were from Boston. That's not so far from Maine. How come this is your first year at camp?"

Sharon laughed. "It's a wonder I even got here this year. Mother thinks I should do one thing, Grandmother thinks something else. And Grandfather — well, he just waits to see what happens next!"

Susan looked thoughtful. "What's your mother like?"

"Oh, Mother's great!" Sharon smiled. "She's awfully pretty. I guess I must take after my dad. Was your mother pretty?"

"Fabulous. Absolutely fabulous. Daddy used to have her picture on his desk, and then — " she broke off.

"And then what?" Sharon asked.

"Well, he caught me looking at it and it's never been around since." Susan punched her pillow. "Want to go with me to the commissary for that popsicle?" she asked.

Sharon stood motionless. She stared at Susan.

"Well. How about it?" Susan spoke impatiently. "What are you staring at?"

Sharon's voice trembled. She held out her arm. "Look! Goosebumps!"

"What do you mean?" Susan sat up on her cot.

"Don't you feel it?" Sharon asked. "Don't you know what's happening? Don't you think it's peculiar that we both look so much alike and — and have the same, identical birthdays?"

Susan stretched, and shrugged. "Oh, that! Well, it's just one of those things, I guess."

Sharon shook her head. "Not when I have goose-bumps! Mother always says I'm psychic. You know — that I can sense things when something strange is going to happen!"

Susan laughed. "Oh, Sharon! Come on!"

Sharon whirled away. She ran to the chest of drawers. Swiftly she turned back. "Look. Look at this!" Her hand shook.

Susan stepped back. "I — I don't understand. *What are you doing with her picture?*"

"It's my mother," Sharon answered, her voice trembling.

"But it's *my* mother. It's the same picture Daddy had on his desk!"

Sharon dropped to the edge of her cot. "That's what I mean, Susan," she said quietly. "Don't you see?"

Susan reached for the photograph. She didn't look at Sharon. "Why don't you go have lunch? It's too late for popsicles, anyhow," she said. Her voice was trembling.

"How can you think of food at a time like this!" Sharon exclaimed.

Both of Susan's hands struck at the cot mattress. "Oh, *go*. For goodness' sake, Sharon, please *go!*"

Without another word Sharon started for the door. As she stepped away from the cabin she heard Susan. She was sobbing brokenheartedly. Sharon hesitated. Then she hurried away down the path.

The Plan

IT WAS A DAY LATER. Susan scooped the last pad-dleful of ice cream from the paper cup. She reached over and picked up Sharon's from the floor. "Demerits, campers!" she imitated Miss Inch. "Let's keep our cabins clean!"

"Why, Miss Inch!" Sharon giggled. "How your voice has changed! And your shape too!"

Susan dropped the cups in the wastepaper basket, then sat down saddle-style on the straight-backed chair. She clasped the back and rested her chin on her hands. "Sharon — you know, I've been wondering. How do you suppose it happened? I mean — Daddy and me living in California, and you and Mother in Boston?"

"My goodness, Susan — I don't know. In fact, I can't even imagine!"

"Well, I can!" Susan said firmly. "Gosh! I can imagine it right now! There we were — only a year old. Probably we could hardly sit up alone! Maybe they had a big quarrel. And maybe Mother said, 'I want this one — you can have the other.' And Dad said 'O.K., but just don't call that one Evers!' "

Sharon's eyes filled with tears. "I'll never believe that — not in a million years!"

"Then, what's your idea?"

Sharon frowned. "Well," she began, "I see it this way. I imagine they had a dreadful quarrel — and they just couldn't make up afterward. Probably Mother packed us both up to leave the ranch, and then — then she just couldn't be mean enough to leave Dad without his half. So, she just hated it, but she had to let him pick you." She wiped her eyes. "How do you suppose I feel being the one who didn't get picked?"

Susan flung her arms around her sister. "Oh, Sharon! You nut!" She burst out laughing. "We're both nuts. We don't know a thing about it."

"We know one thing," Sharon said quietly. "Neither one of them ever married anybody else."

"Well, what does that mean?"

"Secretly — in their innermost hearts — they must be still in love."

Susan blinked. "I don't get it. I think your poetry book is going to your head. Why would they stay apart all these years if they were in love?"

"All true lovers have a simply dreadful time," Sharon

answered. "History is jammed with them. Look at Romeo and Juliet!"

"Where?" Susan looked around.

"Now who's the nut? They were famous lovers, silly. And they had a terrible time." Sharon moved over to the cot and sat down.

Suddenly Susan pushed out of the chair. "Sharon! I've got it!"

"What? Got what?"

Susan whirled in a circle. "Oh, my gosh! What if — Oh! It's just so scary. But we might be able to pull it off!"

"Stop jumping. What's so scary? What could we pull off?"

Susan jumped on the cot. "You want to know Father. I'm just dying to know Mother. Well, we could — could switch places."

"Switch places?"

"Sure!" Sue bounced up and down. "We're twins, aren't we? Oh!" She stretched out her arms. "I'm getting goosebumps now!"

Sharon jumped up. "Oh, we could. And there's more to it than just switching places, Susan!"

"What?"

Sharon clapped her hands together. "If we switched, sooner or later, they'd have to unswitch us. Don't you see. They'd have to meet again! Oh, Susan. I believe fate brought us together!"

Susan swung Sharon around the cabin. "And we'd bring *them* together. Just having to unmix us, they'd have to meet!"

"We'll have to plan!" Sharon exclaimed. "Step one and step two — like that!"

"When do we start?" Susan laughed.

"Well, not until after lunch anyhow," Sharon giggled. "Come on. Let's make the dining hall in time for seconds!"

Susan sighed loudly. "And all the time I thought you were the poetic one! How can *you* think of food at a time like this?"

It was rest hour, but Sharon sat upright on the straight-backed chair. She kept her eyes closed. Scissors snipped closer and closer to her ears. "Aren't you getting it awfully short, Sue?" she asked.

"Nope. I'm checking us both in the mirror. It's exactly like mine. Look!" She bent her head close to Sharon's.

"It's amazing!" Sharon gasped.

"Sure is!" Susan stood back and admired her hair-cutting job.

Sharon patted her head. "You know — it's funny. I *feel* more as though I'm Susan Evers now."

"Well, you don't sound like her," Susan answered. "Remember, Sharon, try not to sound too Boston. Daddy and Hecky will just about fall over if you come out with those 'shawn'ts' and 'cawn'ts.'" She spread out her hands. "Besides, if I could give up biting my finger-nails to fool Mother, you ought to be able to talk Western for Dad."

Sharon nodded. "Gosh! Do you realize that by this time tomorrow you'll be in Boston?"

"And you'll be zooming over the whole U. S.!" Susan said. "Now let's go over this once more. What's my horse's name?"

"Schatzie."

"Dog?"

"Andromeda."

"Right. And remember to thank Verbena for fixing chili beans. She's sure to have them first thing, because they're my absolute favorite food."

"I will. And I'll bite my nails — but not until just before the plane lands." Sharon shuddered, and looked at her fingers. "Poor nails!"

"And chew gum — often! I do."

Sharon laughed. "And you chew gum seldom — if ever. Now, let's do your part. Where is your bedroom at Mother's?"

"Second floor. Second door on left."

"The library and the music room are on the first floor. Which way is the music room?"

"Right, as you come in the front door."

Sharon frowned. "You know, that's the only thing that has me worried. Gran's apt to ask you to play the piano — and she isn't going to expect 'Chopsticks,' either!"

"Oh, I can put Band-Aids on a couple of fingers. That's nothing to worry about. What I'm worrying about is your riding Schatzie."

"Why? Is he very spirited?"

"I'm thinking more about the way you ride. Hecky will wonder if something's wrong with you if you begin hopping up and down in the saddle. He never heard of Eastern style posting. Just *sit*."

"Susan, what if we're both flops?"

"Oh, for goodness' sake! Then we'll just get unmixed that much sooner. Don't worry. Remember, the big thing is to get Mother and Dad together."

"It sure is," Sharon sighed. "And at the ranch, too. Boston is no place for a romance — at least, not our old house! Well, I guess I'd better get my popsicle stick birdcage ready for you to give to Gran. I promised her a present from arts and crafts class. Don't you think I ought to have something to give to Dad?"

"Oh, I made a braided leather belt you can give him," Susan answered. She giggled. "How about giving Dad the popsicle stick birdcage and giving Gran the braided leather belt?"

"Susan! Honestly! That's what I worry about. You just aren't *Boston*. What a crazy idea! Really!"

Closing day was an exciting bustle of activity. Station wagons were parked up and down the dirt road. Parents arrived to carry their daughters back home. Counselors hurried about being helpful. Campers ran around saying good-bye until next summer.

Susan and Sharon stood together exchanging last-minute advice.

"Remember, Susan — get Mother talking about how she met Daddy, and about their first date. That's sure to be important."

"Sharon!" Miss Inch called. "Your chauffeur is waiting for you, dear."

Together the girls started walking toward Miss Inch. "Anyhow, if we're in real trouble we can always phone each other," Sharon said. "Don't forget that I'm calling you at one a.m. Boston time tonight."

Miss Inch looked at the twins. "Well, good-bye to one of the look-alikes! I know the punishment was harsh, girls. But you've survived. Perhaps you have even learned something from the experience."

"Oh, boy! Have we!" Susan exclaimed. "You'd be surprised, Miss Inch!"

Miss Inch smiled at her. "Well, good-bye, Sharon. We'll see you next summer."

Susan smiled back. "Good-bye, Miss Inch. I *cawn't* tell you how much I've enjoyed my stay."

The girls turned to walk down to the road, where Staimes, the chauffeur, waited. "We'd better say good-bye right here," Sharon said, stopping suddenly. "We don't want Staimes to think he's seeing double!" She kissed Susan. "Good-bye, twin! And no *shawn't, cawn't, awn't.* I promise!"

Susan laughed. "That reminds me. Here's your going-away present." Something was pressed into Sharon's hand. Susan ran to the car. "Good-bye!" She waved back.

When the big car disappeared around the bend in the dirt road, Sharon looked at her present. Neatly wrapped in tissue paper and decorated with Lake Nakimquam pine cones, were six packages of chewing gum!

18 Belgrave Square

Staimes pulled the car up to the curb. "Well, here we are, miss. Home again!"

Susan stared hard at the entrance of 18 Belgrave Square. At the top of a short, steep flight of steps was the big door Sharon had described. It was all just as Sharon had said it would be — tall windows, rosy old brick, and ivy framing each window in dark, leafy greenery. Hurriedly Susan put away the notebook of "reminders" Sharon had given her. She reached for the popsicle stick birdcage on the seat beside her. "Well, here goes nothing," she muttered, stepping to the sidewalk.

"Beg pardon, miss?" Staimes asked.

Susan swallowed. She waggled the birdcage in her hand. "I was just saying — this seems like nothing."

Staimes smiled. "Oh, it's a fine cage. Your grandmother will be very pleased." They walked up the high front steps.

At the door Susan took a deep breath. "In just a minute," she told herself, "for the first time in my whole life, I'll be saying 'hello, Mother.'" She stepped quickly into the house.

Cool. Quiet. *Stiff*. "Golly!" she breathed. "No wonder Sharon doesn't chew gum! This is sure different from the ranch!" Before her, richly colored rugs made rectangles of color on the polished floor. Twinkling crystal prisms hung from candlelike wall lamps above the antique mahogany tables placed at either side of partly opened, big white double doors. The library! Susan heard a cool, firm voice from beyond the doors. "Now, I'll want all the gilt chairs in the music room. See that they are well dusted."

Grandmother McKendrick! It must be! That chilly voice couldn't be Mother's!

"Who is that I hear out there?"

Susan whirled. It was Grandfather! — silvery-haired, shorter than her father, and dimples! Sharon hadn't mentioned dimples.

"Is that my little girl? Could that tall, gangly person possibly be Sharon McKendrick?" Grandfather McKendrick held out his arms.

Quickly Susan ran to him. "Hi, Grandfather!" They hugged each other.

"Here! Here! Let me look at you. Have you had your — what's the matter, dear?" He tucked his hand under her chin. Susan sniffed his coat. "Say, young lady! What are you doing?" he laughed.

"Making a memory." Susan's voice was muffled.
"A memory?"

"Uh huh. Years and years from now, I'm going to remember how my grandfather always smells wonderful — all peppermint and tobacco!"

Grandfather McKendrick chuckled. "Well, the peppermint is for my indigestion, and the tobacco is to make your grandmother mad." They laughed together.

"Sharon!"

Before Susan looked up, she knew she'd see her mother standing on the curving staircase. But the photograph had not prepared her for the tall, graceful woman who paused, her hand on the banister.

"*Mother!*"

"Welcome home, darling!" Margaret McKendrick started on down the stairs. "Oh, it's good to have you home. Let me take a look at you. *Sharon!* What on earth have you done to your hair?"

"Cut it."

"Well, that's easy to see. Oh, well. It will grow again." She looked closely at Susan. "What's the matter, Sharon? Are those tears?"

Susan blinked quickly. "I can't help it, Mother. If you only knew!"

"Why, Sharon! When did you arrive?" Grandmother McKendrick came briskly out of the library. She wore a plum-colored suit, and her hair lay in smooth, silver-touched waves, close to her head. Sharon felt a pang of disappointment. "I wish she could have been sort of dimply, like Grandfather," she thought.

"What have you done to your hair, child?"

"She cut it," her mother answered for her.

"If my opinion means anything in this house, which I doubt, I like it short. I like it the way it is," Grandfather said, his eyes twinkling.

"Mercy, Charles!" Grandmother said to her husband, "Do stop burbling. Do go read your newspaper!"

Grandfather McKendrick chuckled. He winked quickly at Susan. "Well, dear. You see, I'm in disgrace with your grandmother! I'll see you at dinner." He walked away.

"My gosh!" Susan thought. "I wonder how they ever let Sharon out of sight. You'd think it was *their* hair!" Then she remembered the birdcage and held it out to her grandmother.

"This is the present Sharon made for you." What a dumb thing to have said! Her cheeks turned crimson.

Grandmother McKendrick held it up. "Now don't tell me the latest thing at girls' camps is baby talk! 'Sharon made it' indeed! What is it, dear?"

Susan almost gasped in relief at her grandmother's words. "I'll have to be awfully careful every second," she thought. Aloud, she said, "It's a birdcage. Made of popsicle sticks."

"Did you eat that many or did other campers provide them for you?" Grandmother McKendrick smiled. She kissed Susan. "Thank you, dear," she said.

"Come upstairs with me, Sharon," her mother said. "We can have a chat while I finish dressing."

Thankfully Susan followed her mother up the stairs. "About one person at a time is about all I can manage, yet," she thought.

Susan leaned against a bedpost and watched her mother loop the beautiful flowing red hair into a knob. Nobody she knew wore her hair that way. She thought of some of Dad's dates who occasionally visited at the ranch. Mother looked — well, old-fashioned, in a beautiful sort of way.

"Did you make some nice friends at camp?" her mother asked.

"Oh, yes. One girl in particular."

"From Boston?"

"Oh, no. Just from someplace." Susan walked over to the dressing-table and looked at her mother's reflection in the mirror.

Her mother put down the hairbrush. "Sharon, dear. *Why* are you staring? You look as if you've never seen me before!"

Susan flushed. "Oh, I don't know. I'm just happy that I'm here and you're here, and — and you're *you!*"

Her mother arose and kissed her lightly. "Well, I'm happy that you're here and that you're *you!* Now, be a good girl and zip me up." She turned. Susan ran the zipper up its track and patted her mother. "Real, real, real!" she sang to herself.

"Margaret!" It was Grandmother looking in the doorway. "Don't forget your Red Cross committee meeting at two thirty. We'll meet at the Somerset after I finish with my garden club. Yes?"

"Yes, Mother. See you later."

The door closed.

"Mother!" Susan cried out. "You're going *out?*"

Her mother looked at her, puzzled. "Why, what's the

42

matter, Sharon dear? I've never seen you like this be-fore!"

"Well, I just got here," Susan said. "I thought we'd spend the day together and just talk."

Her mother frowned. "Sharon, you know I can't can-cel Red Cross."

Susan thought quickly. With Mother and Grand-mother both gone, goodness knows what might hap-pen! What if Grandfather said, "Sharon, I've missed hearing you play the piano. Give us a tune!" Susan shuddered. She swung around the bedpost. "Well, it's just that I wanted to write to Stafford this afternoon, and I thought I should ask your advice first," she said.

"Stafford? Now who is Stafford?" her mother asked.

"Oh, he's a darling boy I met at camp."

Her mother pulled on white gloves. "Well, I'll be glad to give you whatever advice I can, dear. What is the problem?"

Susan thought fast. What would be a really *good* problem? A problem good enough to make her mother take those white gloves off? "Well," she began, "actually, marriage. You see, Stafford thinks waiting for years is silly. I just thought I ought to ask how long you waited before you married."

"*Sharon!*"

Susan hated to see the shocked look in her mother's blue eyes, but it was worth it. Slowly her mother drew off the gloves.

"This has been a wonderful picnic, darling," Margaret McKendrick smiled at Susan and leaned back against the tree trunk. "I guess the Red Cross *could* get along without me for just this once!"

Susan looked guiltily at the tips of her shoes. "Well, I guess Stafford maybe wasn't important enough to miss a meeting for. To be perfectly frank, Mother, the old zing just wasn't there."

"Zing?"

"Yes. You know — the charge that shoots up your spine when you meet the one man you want to marry. Like when you met Daddy." She looked quickly into her mother's eyes. "What was Daddy like, Mother?"

Her mother crumpled a paper cup. "I don't know how we got around to *him*," she said.

"I guess people don't like the idea of talking about somebody they've once been in love with, do they?"

"Oh, Sharon! It was many, many years ago. Don't dramatize it."

"O.K.," Susan replied. Then, "Did he take you someplace on your very first date?"

"Certainly! Especially on our very first date. That's what young men do, dear — they make a plan for the girl's pleasure."

"Mm." Susan thumped her heel against a tree root. "Well, where did you go?"

"Oh — one of those little Italian restaurants. It was in New York City, not Boston."

"Was it nice?"

Susan's mother closed her eyes. She smiled. "Very nice. Checkered tablecloths. Drippy candles. I think it was called 'Martinelli's.' "

"Was there music? I mean, 'they're playing our song' type of thing?"

Her mother's eyes opened. She hurriedly rose to her feet. "Goodness, time flies! We must be starting back."

Susan carried the picnic basket. Her mother's arm rested comfortably around her shoulders. They walked slowly across the soft grass of the park — the Common, Sharon had called it. "I'll never get any wedding bells to start ringing at *this* speed," Susan thought, unhappily. "Mother didn't even remember the music!"

Just then her ears caught the sound of low humming. She glanced up quickly. There was a happy, faraway look in Margaret McKendrick's eyes. " *'For now! For always,'* " she began to sing softly.

Susan held her breath. "It's their song! I just know it is! I *have* taken step one!" she thought excitedly.

The Ranch

"Susan said there was a pool. But I never expected this!" Sharon almost said it aloud — for there it lay — all one hundred feet of it — sparkling blue-green under the California sun. Along its edge was a broad terrace with yellow and white umbrellas shading the tables and gaily flowered chairs. And the ranch house! Sharon clapped her hands together in delight! "It's perfectly beautiful!" she gasped.

Her father laughed as he lifted the luggage from the convertible. "Well, it's all about the same. You didn't think it was going to change, did you?" He looked toward the house. "Get ready! Here comes the welcoming committee."

Sharon turned. A tall motherly woman was hurrying out of the door — Verbena! And there was Hecky, a regular cowboy, coming around the corner of the house. And barking a noisy welcome, a big police dog bounded toward them from the direction of the stables. Andromeda, of course!

But nothing jotted down in the notebook could have helped Sharon through what happened next! Andromeda came to a skidding stop. There was a low growl. "Hi, Andromeda!" Sharon said doubtfully.

Verbena rushed up. "Hello, honey! Give me a hug!" She kissed Sharon warmly. "Andromeda! Stop that! Well, did you ever! Sakes alive! If Andromeda isn't acting as though Susan is a stranger!"

"Silly dog!" Sharon said, weakly.

To her relief, Hecky called out, "Hey! What have you got there, Mitch?"

"Oh, I found this girl hanging around the airport. Thought I might as well bring her along," her father called back.

Hecky strode up. "Hi, darlin'!" He tousled her hair.

"Hi, Hecky." Sharon reached up to smooth her bangs back into place. *Susan wouldn't do that!* Quickly, she lowered her hands, but not before Verbena noticed.

"I do believe our wild Comanche is takin' pains with her looks." Verbena laughed, but there was a puzzled frown between her gray eyes.

"Well," Sharon said uneasily, "guess I'll go up to my room."

"Chili beans for dinner, honey," her father called. "And hurry. There's someone I want you to meet."

In the brightly colored bedroom, Sharon pulled on a pair of Susan's blue jeans. She reached in a drawer and found a striped shirt. So far she hadn't forgotten any of Susan's instructions. "Thank goodness I studied the notes!" Sharon thought, as she pulled the shirt over her head. She looked into the mirror. "Verbena, do you think I should have put on a dress, instead?"

Verbena shook out a rumpled skirt from the suitcase and hung it in the closet. She laughed. "Honey, since when have you been dolling up for dinner around here?"

Sharon flushed. "Well — I just wondered — on account of the company. Was that girl downstairs the 'somebody' Dad wants me to meet?"

Verbena nodded. "I was just thinkin', honey. Why don't you put on your swimming suit? The water will be just fine. Nice and warm, tail-end of the afternoon like it is. Have a swim."

"Good thinking!" Sharon peeled off the shirt. "But who is she? — that girl, I mean."

Verbena slipped a hanger into a dress. "I'm not saying a word. I mind my own business. If your dad wants to make a ninny of himself, that's his affair. I don't say a word!"

Sharon suddenly sat down on the bench before the dressing-table. She stared, wide-eyed, at Verbena. "Verbena! You can't mean — ?"

Verbena bobbed her head up and down. "I do mean! Ridin' together, swimmin' together, out to dinner together! The idea! What does a young girl like that see in him? A man with a grown daughter goin' on fourteen!"

Sharon slowly shook her head. "I don't know."

"Well, I do! A million reasons! And they're all in the

bank — just waitin' for weddin' bells to jiggle them loose!"

"Verbena! No!"

Verbena snorted. "I'm not sayin' a word!" She marched to the bedroom door, then looked back. "But she's awful good with those cool-colored eyes of hers. Look right at you, she can! But it's none of my business. That's why I'm not sayin' a word!"

Sharon watched the door close. Then she lifted the corner of the mattress on Susan's bed and drew out the secret notepad. Yes, thank goodness! She'd written it down. One a.m. in Boston would be ten p.m. in California!

As she came down the staircase she could see her father and the "somebody" on the terrace talking together under a yellow umbrella. Her father's head was bent close to Miss Wedding Bells. Sharon sniffed, "The *last* person I want to see! Well, I can always jump in the pool if I don't want to talk," she thought.

"Hi, Susie!" Her father jumped up. "We were just talking about you — ah — this is Miss Robinson, Susie."

"Call me 'Vicky,' dear," Miss Robinson smiled. "Well, well! I expected a little girl."

"Verbena was right," Sharon thought. "Vicky Robinson's eyes look straight at you, and they don't match up with that smile."

"Hi," she said, aloud.

There was a flat silence. "How about drinks, everybody?" Her father said, jumping up. "Ginger ale, Coke, root beer, Susie? What'll it be?"

"Ginger ale, thank you." She watched her father

stride off into the house, then quickly picked up a large rubber duck at the edge of the pool. "Well, excuse me. Guess I'll take the plunge."

"Oh, wait, dear! I — I wanted to tell you something. Can you keep a secret?" Vicky asked.

"From whom?"

"From your father."

Sharon tossed the duck into the pool and watched it bob upright. "Oh," she said coolly, "in that case, you'd better not tell me, then." She dived into the water and quickly bobbed up to the surface. "Daddy and I just don't keep secrets," she called loudly back to Vicky. "We tell each other everything!" She was pleased to see her father's guest scowl.

Vicky leaned forward. "I merely wanted to say" — she broke off. "Come closer, dear. I can't shout."

Sharon stroked to the edge of the pool. "Yes?"

"I merely wanted to say — I think your father is a very wonderful kind of person!" Vicky smiled.

"Oh." Sharon reached for the duck. "Don't worry about that, Vicky. That's no secret. All of his girls say that!"

Vicky stared. The smile disappeared. "*All* of his girls?"

"Well, I guess so. At least all of them who come up here say that. You know — first one, then another."

Her father came through the doorway, balancing a tray in his hands. "Well, how are you two getting on?" He set the tray on the table. "Getting to know each other?" he asked.

Vicky beamed at him. "Indeed we are! We've had a lovely little talk!"

Sharon pushed the duck along the pool edge. She laughed. "Daddy, it was the funniest thing — wasn't it, Vicky? We understood each other practically immediately!"

The smile froze on Vicky's face. Her cold eyes looked icily into Sharon's.

At 1:02 a.m. the telephone rang in the McKendrick library. Susan snatched it up at the first ring. "Hello?" she said, softly.

"Susan? Sharon. How's everything?"

"Oh, Sharon! Mother's the absolute living end! Gorgeous! Breathtaking! And can you believe it? I know all about the first date! Italian dinner, music — everything — and — "

"Susan, stop! Will you listen!"

"And their song goes like this," Sue began singing: "For now. For al-ways — !"

"Susan, listen. I've got something to tell you. It's serious."

"Oh?"

"We're in trouble. You'll have to bring Mother out here *immediately*."

Susan moved forward to the very edge of her grandfather's desk chair. "Holy Smokes, Sharon, what are you talking about? I've just had one *day* with Mother. Gosh! I hardly got to know her at all!"

"Susan, it's an emergency! Her name is Vicky, and she's beautiful. And Dad's serious. He thinks she's wonderful."

There was a pause.

"Susan! Are you there?"

"Sure I'm here. I'm thinking. Look, Sharon, you've got to bust it up."

"I know. That's why you've got to bring Mother!"

"Oh, Sharon, for heaven's sake! You can submarine her! Follow them everywhere!"

"Susan, you've got to tell Mother. Now!"

"No, I won't. You've had her thirteen years and I just got her."

"Susan, please. You don't understand what this means. Please!" Sharon was begging now.

"Not this soon. That's final. Good-bye!"

Slowly Sharon set the phone into its cradle. "What am I going to do? Sue's already started Mother thinking about Daddy," she thought, miserably. "And I can't even begin step one!"

Warning

IT WAS A BEAUTIFUL MORNING. In the distance the Pacific Ocean stretched out beneath the soft blue sky. Sharon, standing with her father on the rolling green of the golf course, watched the smoke trail of a ship at sea. "California certainly is beautiful, isn't it?" she said to her father.

"Say, you've been noticing more about the old home state lately than you have in all your thirteen years." He laughed. "What is this, anyhow?"

"Oh, I don't know," Sharon replied. "Guess I'm just glad to be here and — and everything."

"Well, I'm sure glad you came along today, honey. There's something important I want to talk with you about."

"I want to talk about something too, Daddy."

"Oh? O.K. Go ahead. Let's sit down."

They dropped to the cool grass. Sharon broke off a green blade and twirled it between her fingers.

"Well — shoot!" her father said, leaning back on an elbow.

Sharon drew a deep breath. "Actually — actually, I've been wondering about Mother." There! She'd said it!

Her father sat up. "Your mother! Now what do you want to wonder about something like that for?"

"Well, I do," Sharon answered, firmly. "You know — where she is — things like that."

"How should I know? I lost track. Anyhow, you wouldn't like her."

"Why not?"

"Oh — big staring eyes. Bright red hair. And fat — really fat."

Sharon looked at him coolly. "My goodness, Daddy! I can't imagine how you ever fell in love with her!"

Her father sighed. "Well, you know — you lose your head sometimes. But don't start thinking about her. That was years ago. Besides, you can always talk with me about anything. Always."

Sharon shook her head. "Not always. Sometimes a girl can really *miss* her mother."

"Oh." Her father cleared his throat. "You mean you'd like to talk over certain things with a mother?"

"With my mother." Sharon answered.

Her father reached into his hip pocket and drew out a pipe. Sharon waited. "Well, what do you know! No tobacco!"

There was silence.

"Honey, we could get it straight on one thing, anyhow. Boys." He grinned at Sharon. "I used to be one, you know."

"Oh, that!" Sharon burst out laughing. "Daddy, you're too funny. I've known about all that for simply years."

"Then what are we talking about?" her father asked, a puzzled frown pulling his eyebrows close together.

"Mother," Sharon answered, promptly.

"Oh, that!" Her father stood up. "Look, honey — let's go up to the clubhouse." He picked up his golf bag and turned toward a low rambling building on the hill.

"Score z-e-r-o!" Sharon thought, in disgust. In silence she walked beside her father.

"Hi!" Vicky called. She was seated with an older woman on the clubhouse terrace.

"Listen, Susie — that's Vicky's mother. I expect you to be pleasant and — and ladylike. Come on." Her father quickened his step. Sharon groaned.

"Come right over here to your Auntie Edna!" Vicky's mother, Mrs. Robinson, called out. "Mitch! *This* angelic girl! This is the one you call peanut face?"

Sharon pulled back. Her father's hand pressed her forward. "Oh, Daddy, really!" she muttered.

Mrs. Robinson reached for Sharon's wrist. "Now we're just going to get to know each other!" She turned to her daughter. "Now you and Mitch just run along! Susan and I want to get acquainted. Then after that we'll all have lunch together!"

Sharon looked hard at her father. He hesitated. "Sorry, Edna. I'm afraid we can't today. You see, I promised this day to Susan. We're going to take a ride down the beach."

"I'm terribly sorry," Sharon said politely.

"It's all right, dear. Another time." Mrs. Robinson gushed. "You are adorable!"

Sharon, her hand in her father's, tried to match his long stride as they walked to the car. She could think of nothing to say. "He doesn't look too pleased!" she thought worriedly.

It was a quiet drive back to the ranch. As they turned into the drive, her father said, "I guess Schatzie could stand a little exercise."

"Schatzie! Oh! You meant a *horseback* ride!"

"Susan, what's wrong with you? What other kind of ride would we take on the beach?" Her father looked at her sharply.

Sharon shrugged. She spread out her hands. "Well, I just didn't get that part — beach, I mean. I just heard 'ride.'"

Her father shook his head. "Honest, Susan, sometimes I think something happened to you at that camp!"

"Oh, it did, Daddy! If it hadn't been for Camp Inch, I'd never have — " The sentence came to a dead stop.

"Never have what?"

"Oh! You'll see when I ride Schatzie!"

"See what, for the love of Mike?"

"I don't ride Western anymore. I post. You know — go up and down."

Her father laughed. "Well, that will be interesting to see. I can't wait!"

It was a wonderful ride along the wide beach. The great Pacific combers rolled up and crashed in a flood of foam, then sucked back, leaving the beach like a sand mirror to be galloped across.

As they rode slowly back to the ranch Sharon was quiet. All this would be lost forever unless she could make the plan work. And time was running out.

"Hey! I asked you a question," her father said.

"Oh? Sorry, Daddy. I didn't hear." They reached the ranch gate. Sharon slipped off Schatzie and climbed up to the top bar. "What did you ask?"

Her father rode up beside her. "I said, 'What do you think of Vicky?'"

"Oh. Her." Sharon thumped the lower bar with her heels. "In what respect?" she asked.

"What respect? Why, as a person, of course!"

Sharon jumped down from the gate. "Daddy, I really couldn't say. She's a perfect stranger to me." She looked up at her father. "I'll race you to the house!" Swiftly she swung back the big gate and climbed on Schatzie again. She gave the little mare a light spank with the rein end. They were off!

"Susan! Hey! Wait a minute!" her father called. "I'm not through talking to you!"

Sharon didn't stop until Schatzie reached the stable door. She tossed the bridle reins to Hecky, and looked back to see if her father had followed. He hadn't, but she saw that a car had stopped down by the gate. As she watched, her father got off his horse. He walked to the car, bent forward — and kissed Vicky.

Slowly Sharon walked over to the kitchen steps. She sat down. "Oh, he can't!" she said aloud. "He just *can't!*"

The screened door behind her slammed. Verbena came down the steps. Quietly she sat down beside Sharon. "Honey, you used to confide in me. Anything you want to talk over?"

Sharon shook her head.

"You wouldn't like to tell me why you don't like chili beans so much anymore, or why you've taken to hanging up your clothes real neat, or why your own dog never comes near you?"

Sharon jumped up. "Oh, dear Verbena! You're a mystic!"

"Mystic? Well, I'm no mystic, whatever that may be. But there is somethin' mighty strange goin' on around here. Are you *sure* you don't want to tell me somethin'?"

"Tell you what?" Sharon asked.

Verbena shook her head. "Honey, I don't know. It's almost as if you were — well, no. That's impossible!"

"Almost as if I were who, Verbena?" Sharon asked quietly.

"Forget it, honey. Never mind."

Sharon took a big breath. "You mean — as if I were *Sharon?*"

Verbena nodded.

"Oh, Verbena! I've got to tell somebody. Would you swear you'd never tell Daddy? *Promise?*"

"Susan!" Sharon's father came around the corner of the house. "Why'd you go running off like that? I want to talk with you just a minute."

Verbena turned to the kitchen door. "Hmph! He didn't know what a good thing he had when he had it!" She slammed the door.

"Now, what's got into her?" Sharon's father exclaimed. "Come on. Let's walk around to the living room."

Sharon trailed behind her father. He settled himself comfortably in a big chair. She walked over to the piano and sat down. "I'm listening," she said.

"Well, first of all, honey — about me. You probably think of me as your father."

"Oh, I do, Daddy!" Sharon struck a chord softly.

"What I mean is — you think of me as ancient and old."

"I don't think you're at all ancient!" Sharon ran her fingers rapidly over the keys.

"Certainly I'm not," said her father. "Say, where'd you learn to play the piano like that?"

Sharon turned pink. " — er — they taught us a special way at camp."

"That's pretty good for five weeks! Now what was I saying?"

"That you aren't ancient." Sharon began banging out "Chopsticks."

"Cut it out, honey. I can't think. Pay attention." Sharon turned to face him.

"Now then! I want to have this little talk with you about making Vicky a part of our family." He stood up.

"Daddy!" Sharon jumped to her feet. She threw her arms around her father and pressed her face into his shirtfront. "It's a wonderful idea! I've always wanted to have a sister." Her voice was muffled.

"Honey, I can't hear you. Did you say 'sister'?"

Sharon bobbed her head.

"But, peanut, you're missing the point!"

Sharon pushed back. "Oh, Daddy, you're *sweet* to want to adopt her!"

Her father flushed red. "No, baby," he said, "I want to marry her."

"*Marry* her!"

Her father nodded.

"Daddy! You've just got to be kidding! You can't marry her. Why, she's just a girl. Compared to her — why Daddy, you're an old man!"

"I am not!" her father said, his face redder than ever.

"You are *too!*"

"Don't shout!"

Sharon turned away. When she spoke, her voice trembled. "You can't get married, Daddy. It would just ruin everything. All the planning, and all the maps. Why, I even made a map of the bedroom!"

Her father's hands were on her shoulders. He turned her to face him.

"What are you talking about?"

Sharon pushed his hands away. Her blue eyes blazed. "I cut my hair for you! Look at it! And you! You just take my fingernails for granted — and I've been *biting* them for you! Nothing but days and days of practicing — " She broke off. Vicky entered the room.

"Vicky, I don't know what's wrong with her. I just begin to talk and she gets hysterical. She isn't making any sense!" He looked from one to the other.

"Well, let me have a talk with her, darling. Women understand these things better. Make yourself scarce."

Sharon ran from the room.

Two hours later, Vicky's car was still parked in the drive. Sharon looked down from the bedroom window. She sighed. "Well, I might as well get it over with." She walked rapidly toward the bedroom door, and without slowing her pace, ran down the stairs. Vicky sat in the living room.

"Hello, darling," she said, watching Sharon walk into the room. "I'm afraid this came as quite a shock to you, didn't it? Men put things so badly."

Sharon sat down.

Vicky patted the couch cushion beside her. "Come over here and talk to me. You're not afraid, are you?"

Sharon arose. "I'm not afraid to talk to anybody." She settled into the couch corner.

"You're a big girl now, Susan. Why, you're old enough to understand about falling in love — "

Sharon gritted her teeth together. Ugh! How long would this go on?

" — and with someone gentle and mature, rough-edged, but quick to laugh, someone understanding and wise — all the things I've come to love and cherish in your father." Vicky paused. She fluttered her eyelashes at Sharon.

"Well, that's very refreshing, I must say!" Sharon said,

calmly. "Most girls just run after Daddy because he's so wealthy." She smiled sweetly.

Vicky's eyes narrowed. Her lips pressed into a firm line. "Look, pet, I've tried to be friendly, but I'm going to marry your father. So you get used to the idea." She stood up.

"You want to bet?" Sharon asked, still smiling.

"Don't tangle with me, honey. You'll be in way over your head!" Vicky spun angrily on her heel and marched out of the room.

Shocking News

GRANDMOTHER McKENDRICK FROWNED. "Who on earth could be sending that child a telegram!" She glanced at the library clock. "And at this hour of night — it's nine o'clock!"

"May I read it, Sharon?" Her mother held out her hand. Susan passed the telegram along.

"Alexander Graham one a.m. important," she read aloud. "What does it mean, Sharon?" She handed it back.

"Oh, it's this girl in California I met at camp. She's crazy about this boy, Alexander. She had this important date and didn't get home until one a.m." Susan pushed nervously at her bangs.

"Don't do that, dear." Her mother reached over and smoothed the bangs.

"Never heard of such a thing! A child Sharon's age out at that hour! Outrageous!" Grandmother McKendrick said.

"My goodness!" Susan said. "This evening has passed so quickly — playing chess, and everything. I guess it's time for me to go upstairs." She kissed her grandfather.

"Don't you feel well?" asked her mother.

"Oh, fine. Well, good night everybody." She scooted from the room.

"It is going to be a very full day," Grandmother McKendrick said, next morning at the breakfast table. She stirred sugar into her coffee. "Now, Sharon, you have your dancing lesson at ten thirty. From there you might as well go straight on to Leonardo Hall for the music appreciation course. After that, Staimes can drive you to — "

"I don't believe I'll be able to do any of those things today," Susan said.

"Why, Sharon! You interrupted your grandmother!"

"Well, I have something important to tell you."

Grandmother McKendrick's eyebrows lifted. "What did you say?"

Susan looked toward her grandmother a moment then turned to her mother. "I want to tell you that I think what you and Daddy did to us children is terrible!"

"Sharon!" her mother gasped.

"In fact," Susan went on, determinedly, "I think it is simply lousy!"

"Sharon!"

"And we might as well get it straight. I'm *not* Sharon. I'm *Susan*."

Margaret McKendrick stared in thunderstruck horror.

"Impossible!" Grandmother McKendrick exclaimed.

Susan turned to her grandmother. "No, it isn't impossible, Gran. We met at camp and we decided to switch places. Grandfather knows. He heard us talking last night on the phone."

"One a.m., Alexander Graham *Bell*," said her grandfather, nodding.

"Henry!" Grandmother McKendrick gasped. "Why didn't — "

Susan interrupted. "And you might as well all know — Sharon is at the ranch with Daddy in California.

She's swimming and she's riding *my* horse, and she's having a perfectly keen time! And I'm stuck with these old music lessons — and I *hate* them!" She looked at her mother.

Margaret McKendrick stared, white-faced. "Susan!" she said, in almost a whisper.

"I'm sorry, Mother." Susan's voice shook. "But I wanted to see you. I *missed* not having a mother. I just hoped maybe you could love me as *me* — not Sharon. I — I love *you!*"

"Oh, *Susan!*" Margaret McKendrick pushed back her chair. She rushed to Susan. "Susan *darling!*" Her arms held Susan tight.

In the library a short while later, Margaret McKendrick paced nervously back and forth.

Grandfather McKendrick glanced at her irritably over his newspaper. "Margaret! You're pacing like a caged tiger! If you must stalk around, I wish you would find some other place in this house to do it."

His daughter paid no attention to him. Her mind was on her own daughters. "Of course, Father, Susan will have to be returned to Mitch at once!"

"Of course," her father agreed. "Just like a package sent back to the post office — no such person at this address!"

"Father!"

"Well, that's how it sounds."

"You know I can't do anything else. Legally, she's his."

Her father nodded. "Yes, indeed. Put her on a plane — that's all there is to it!"

Margaret hesitated. "Well — er — I have in mind taking her myself."

"Oh?"

"Well, I wouldn't want either of the girls traveling alone. And, of course, I'd be bringing Sharon back with me."

"Certainly. *She's* legally yours."

Margaret's eyes filled with tears. "Like the 'His' and 'Her' bath towels — that's what Susan said."

Grandfather McKendrick stood up. "Well, my dear. If you're determined to take the child West, I'd better go and make your travel arrangements. Are you planning to leave immediately?"

"Well, of course, immediately. Why would I want to delay the trip?"

"Oh, I don't know. I thought probably you'd have things like shopping to do first."

"Shopping! At a time like this?"

"Well, no. I don't suppose you would. You're right. Perfectly right." He walked to the library door, then turned. "I have to hand it to you, Margaret. You do have character! Now take the average woman — she'd be running around saying she had nothing suitable to wear and that her hair looked awful. That sort of thing."

He opened the door. "As I said, it certainly does show character not to go along with the new fashion trends in clothing and hair styles." His dimples showed briefly. "Well, I'll be hurrying along. I wonder what kind of wife Mitch has now. Oh well. When you get there, say hello to Mitch for me." The door closed.

For a moment Margaret McKendrick stood motionless. Then her hand went up and touched her neatly pinned hair. She patted it thoughtfully.

"Mother? You in here?" Susan opened the door.

Her mother smiled. "Susan, what do you say to a stopover in New York City before we go to California? We could have a few days together, do some shopping — things like that."

Susan threw her arms around her mother. "Oh, Mother! I was just *praying* you'd come with me!"

Strange Homecoming

FOUR DAYS LATER a joyful reunion took place in front of the ranch house.

"I declare!" Verbena exclaimed. "If it wasn't for Susan bein' in her travelin' clothes and Sharon, here, wearing her jeans, I wouldn't know *who* it was I just kissed 'hello' to!"

Margaret McKendrick laughed. "Isn't it amazing, Verbena?"

Verbena brushed away a tear. "It sure is! Say, it's wonderful to see you here again, Mrs. Evers."

The twins' mother flushed with pleasure. "Thank you, Verbena. Has Sharon been behaving herself?"

"Oh, Mother!" Sharon picked up her mother's suitcase. "Come on, Susan. Let's get Mother's things upstairs."

"O.K.," Susan replied. She turned to Verbena. "Where's Daddy?"

"He and Hecky went out to look at a calf. They'll be back soon, I guess."

"Well, I'll come right back, then. I'm dying to see him!"

Susan almost jumped up from the chair at the kitchen table when her father walked in the back door. She managed to look calm. "Gosh! I'd better remember who I am now!" she said to herself. She waved, airily. "Hi."

"Well, hi. Look who's talking to me!" her father answered.

Susan looked puzzled. "Why shouldn't I talk to you?"

"Oh, come on, Susan! Don't pretend you don't know

what I'm talking about! You've been walking around like an Egyptian mummy all week!"

"Oh?"

"Yes, 'oh.' Look, I can get married any time I want. Got that?"

"Yeah."

"And not speaking to somebody because you're mad at them is just plain — "

"Feminine." Verbena supplied, coming through the door.

"That's right — feminine."

Verbena marched back out the door.

"And that's the worst part of being feminine, too!" Mitch said, watching the door swing behind Verbena.

"I hear the doorbell," Susan said. "Who's coming?"

"Susie, you *know* who's coming. Vicky and Mrs. Robinson, and Reverend Moseby. And you're to be polite to them. Understand?"

Susan nodded.

"Then come on. Be a nice little hostess. I'll say hello first, then go up and shower."

Mitch hung his jacket over a bedroom chair and sat down to tug off his boots.

"Hi, Dad." Sharon paused in the open doorway. "Did you know your visitors are downstairs?"

"Hi, honey," her father said, absentmindedly. Then he looked up. "Say! What is this?" he asked. "Why aren't you down there with them? Didn't you promise me just now?"

"Oh. Well, I'm just on my way."

"And don't forget to be nice!" her father called after

her. He unbuttoned his shirt and walked into the bathroom. It was filled with steam. A damp bathmat lay crumpled on the floor.

"Now why can't Susie be a little neater?" he thought. "Anything I hate is a messed-up bathroom. Oh, well. At least she's talking to me again. That's something. Now where's my robe?"

In the bedroom across the hall, Margaret McKendrick, fresh from her shower, brushed her damp curls into place. Sharon watched happily. "Just think! I haven't seen you all summer!" She bounced on the bed. "Mother, I just love your haircut!" she exclaimed.

"I love yours too, darling. Susan did a wonderful job." Margaret held up a green silk suit. "Shall I wear this, or do you like the dress with the flowers better?"

Before Sharon could answer, Susan burst in the door. "Hey! Vicky's downstairs. I've been entertaining her. Do you want to see her?"

Sharon yawned lazily. "No thanks," she said in a bored tone. "I've *been* seeing her. For days — and days. Ugh!"

"Who's Vicky?" their mother asked.

The girls looked at each other. Sharon spoke. "Well — er — she's the girl Daddy's going to marry."

"Yeah," Susan nodded. "They're down there now talking about the wedding. You know — should the bride stand here or there, and should they be married inside, or outside by the pool — that sort of thing."

Margaret McKendrick fastened the tasseled belt of Mitch's huge bathrobe. "Well, you two know Vicky but *I* haven't seen her! And I intend to, right now!"

74

"Aren't you going to put on your dress first, Mother?" Sharon asked.

"No. I think your father's robe is just right for this occasion. Come on, Susan."

When her mother and sister left, Sharon hung the green suit and the flowered dress in the closet. "Gosh! Mother's a knockout!" she thought. "New clothes — new haircut. I'll bet Daddy will be just crazy about — "

"Susie?" Mitch, wrapped in a huge striped bath towel, looked around the door.

"Oh, hi, Dad. Want something?"

"Have you seen my robe around here?"

Sharon sat up. "Your *robe?* It's not in here. Why would it be in here?"

"Don't get excited. You took a shower before I did, so — oh well, it will probably turn up."

"Oh, it's sure to!" Sharon answered, beginning to giggle. Quickly she scooped up a pillow and buried her face in it.

"Susan, what's the matter with you?"

"Nothing," the muffled voice came from the pillow depths.

"Then I'd appreciate your going downstairs and staying downstairs until *I* come downstairs! Got it?"

Sharon scrambled off the bed. "Got it, Daddy!" She brushed past him and started down the hall.

"Well, folks," Mitch Evers beamed, a few minutes later. "Everything settled or do you need me in on this?" Clean, shaved, in white flannels, he sauntered across the terrace and joined the group seated by the pool.

"Mitch, dear, as I was just saying to Vicky" — Mrs. Robinson pressed his hand — "the wedding procession will come out from the house over there. Vicky will stand right here. Why, what's the matter, Mitch?"

Mitch Evers was staring toward the trees at the far corner of the terrace. Did his eyes deceive him, or was that . . . "*Maggie!*" he said, under his breath.

"What did you say, dear?" Vicky asked.

Still staring, Mitch took a step backward, and he bent slightly to the left. "Oh, I just thought I saw — that is — "

Before his gaze Maggie and Susan had stepped from around a tree trunk. They both waved cheerily at him.

"What's the matter, Daddy?" Sharon asked.

Her father stared down at her, then toward the big tree. He took another backward step.

Vicky screamed, "Mitch! Watch out!"

Too late. Splash! He was in the pool!

"Are you all right, Mr. Evers?" Reverend Moseby, looking concerned and trying not to smile, hauled at Mitch's jacket.

"Oh, you poor man!" Mrs. Robinson cried.

"Mitch, darling!" Vicky exclaimed.

"Let go, Reverend," Mitch sputtered. "I'm fine. I'll just climb the pool ladder here!"

Sharon held out her hand. "Daddy, you're all wet," she said sweetly.

"Really! Now that's very odd, isn't it?" her father shot back. "Excuse me, folks. I'll just go up and change.

Back in a minute! Back in a minute!" He strode off into the house, squishing water at every step.

Sharon turned to her father's guests. "Excuse me," she said politely. "I'll be right back." She hurried into the living room in time to hear her father say, "*Maggie!*"

Susan was not in sight. Sharon made a speedy turn, and ran into the kitchen. Susan was there, waiting for her.

"Oh, Susan! Do you think it's going to work?" Sharon looked at her twin across the kitchen table.

Susan shook her head. "Gosh, I don't know. Daddy sounded awfully mad when he came into the house."

"Well, he was pretty wet," Sharon said.

Susan groaned. "Wet and mad as a wet hen! Anyhow, after he and Mother began talking in the living room, I left. I didn't think I ought to hang around and listen! After all, it's the first time Daddy's seen Mother in years!"

"That's why I didn't stay," replied Sharon. "It just wouldn't have been *right*."

"Well, maybe we should show up in there now, though. Daddy might as well see both of us at once."

"Yes," Sharon agreed. "It's about time this family got together. Come on!"

"But I don't understand." Mitch looked from Sharon to Susan to Maggie, as the twins stood on either side of their mother in the living room.

"I've been trying to tell you!" Maggie exclaimed.

"The girls met at camp and simply switched places."

"You mean Susie is Sharon, and Sharon is Susie?" Mitch asked, rubbing his forehead.

"No, Daddy," Sharon said. "Susan is Susan, and I'm me. You just *thought* I was Susan." She hesitated. "Are you mad at me?"

A funny look came into her father's eyes. "Mad? Honey, I haven't been mad at you since you made me walk the floor for three hours straight, thirteen years ago. Mad? Aw, honey!"

"Well, I'm grown up now," Sharon answered, "and without a father, I might say!"

"And I'm without a mother," Susan added.

"Daddy, please don't marry that woman!" Sharon begged.

"Girls! Shoo! This can be discussed another time. Run along now! Shoo!" Maggie waved them toward the staircase. "Has everybody forgotten that your father has guests waiting?"

From Susan's bedroom window, a very few minutes later, the girls watched Vicky's convertible go down the drive.

"Boy! Is she mad!" Susan exclaimed.

"How can you tell?"

"Oh, just the way the gravel spurted up from the tires, I guess. She's furious!"

"I think Daddy's furious too," Sharon said in a troubled voice.

"Well, gosh, Sharon! What'd you expect? Having *us* all at once, plus Mother, plus planning a wedding, *plus* taking a dive in the pool!"

"Well, it looks as though we'll never have a Home Sweet Home, the way things are going," Sharon said sorrowfully.

"We've got to think. We can't give up now. Gosh, we're already all the way up to step three."

"Which one is that?" Sharon asked, staring out the window.

"Romance. Remember you said 'Get her away from Boston.' Well, I did it. She's here and we're here. Now what's next?"

Sharon turned from the window. She stuck out her arm. "Look! Goosebumps!"

Susan straightened *her* arm. "Goosebumps! Are you thinking what I'm thinking?"

"Their first date at Martinelli's? Checkered table-cloths — candles — gypsy violin music!"

"Yeah! It's gotta be tonight. Come on. We need Verbena and Hecky to help us on this."

They hurried downstairs to the kitchen.

Martinelli's-on-the-Terrace

It wasn't easy to get Hecky's promise to dress up as a gypsy and play his fiddle. "I never heard of no gypsy singin' about a Home on the Range," he grumbled.

"If you can't be a gypsy for these kids for just this once," Verbena stormed, "you can get ready to cook your own meals for a month!"

Susan looked up from the cookbook she was studying at the kitchen table. "Verbena, do we have any veal?" she asked.

"It so happens we do. Why?"

"Well, here's a recipe that sounds *very* Italian — veal par-miggi-onni."

"Par-me-johnny. Get it right." Verbena looked over Susan's shoulder at the recipe.

"O.K. Parmejohnny. Could you fix it?"

"I don't know why not."

Sharon turned to Hecky. "We've got to have atmosphere. You know — like fancy little restaurants in New York. Hecky, do we have anything we could hang up on the terrace? Something drapey?"

Hecky scratched his head. "How about them Navajo blankets in the bunkhouse, Verbena?"

"Swell!" Susan jumped up and clapped her hands. "They'd be beautiful!"

"What are you kids going to do for your part in this?" Hecky asked.

"What do you mean, Hecky?" Sharon looked puzzled.

"Well, now, don't tell me a fancy New York restaurant wouldn't have a floor show!"

"Gosh! Hecky's right! I never thought of that!" Sue said. "We've got to have a floor show!"

"Well, let's get busy. We'll have to plan."

Verbena threw up her hands. "Plans, plans. Getting to be nothing but planning going on around here!"

"Verbena!" Mitch called through the kitchen door two hours later. "What's happened with dinner?"

"Dinner's being served on the terrace tonight," Verbena answered, as she counted out napkins.

"Whose idea was that?"

"I don't say a word. It's none of my never-mind. I don't say a word."

"Oh, no, that's right. You never say a word!" Mitch stalked away from the kitchen.

It was a perfect evening. Far, far toward the west, the sun had dipped below the Pacific horizon. The last

golden streak of light was gone, leaving in its place velvety black. Stars glittered above the candlelit terrace.

"Hi, Maggie! Out here!" Mitch called.

Margaret McKendrick stepped from the living room to the terrace. She wore her new flowered frock. "How pretty!" she exclaimed. "What's all this?"

"I don't know. Don't ask *me*." Mitch waved his arms. "It's my house, but nobody ever tells me anything."

They sat down. Verbena, carrying a heavy tray, walked across the terrace.

"Mm. Delicious! What is it?" Maggie asked.

"Veal parmejohnny. That's Italian, you know." Verbena set down the plates and marched off to the kitchen.

"I hate stuff like this. She knows that!" Mitch grumbled.

Hecky, violin in hand, came up to the table. He wore a bright kerchief around his head — like a gypsy, or a pirate — and around his waist was a broad sash.

Mitch stared. "Hecky, what do you think you're doing?"

"I'm a strollin' gypsy, Mitch. Please, Mitch, no comments. I might just kill myself anyhow — I don't know!"

Susan called, "Hecky, it's time!"

Hecky walked away. Maggie picked up a large piece of cardboard.

"What's Verbena left a laundry card on the table for?" Mitch exclaimed.

"Mitch, look! It's a menu." Maggie held it up —

MARTINELLI'S
FINE ITALIAN RESTAURANT

Maggie's voice shook. "Mitch, don't you see? The girls are trying to remind us of our first date!"

"Well, I'll be — why, those sweet, crazy kids!" Mitch Evers said, his voice soft. His eyes blurred suddenly.

At that moment the Navajo blankets swung back to reveal a piano, a record player, and Hecky. He bowed. "The management has gotten together some entertainment for you. Well — ah — without further ado, ladies and gentlemen, I'd like to introduce direct from Boston, playing Beethoven's First Symphony on the piano, Miss Sharon McKendrick."

Maggie and Mitch clapped their hands. Sharon stepped up to the piano and sat down. She began to play. Susan bounced in from behind a blanket, carrying a guitar.

"Will you kindly get off the stage?" Sharon asked. "I'm in the middle of a concert!"

"A concert! You're going to put the customers to sleep!" Susan said. "You gotta get the new sound!" She strummed the guitar. "Come on, let's compromise. You give a little. I'll give a little. Let's get together!"

"Yea, yea, yea," Sharon suddenly sang.

Then they went through a number they had made up an hour before — Sharon playing the piano in a way Grandmother McKendrick would never have approved, Susan playing the guitar, and both singing:

> Two is twice as nice as one.
> Let's get together right away.
> We'll be having twice the fun.
> And you can always count on me.
> A gruesome twosome we will be,
> Let's get together
> Yea, yea, yea!

"That's wonderful, girls!" Maggie clapped.

"Come on down, kids. We've got spaghetti. All kinds of glop," Mitch called cheerily.

"Oh, no, that's all right, thank you. We've had our dinner in the kitchen, haven't we, Sharon?" They sped swiftly into the house.

"Good night, girls! It was lovely!" Maggie called after them.

" 'Night, kids!" called their father.

Before the girls had left, they had turned on the record player. Now it softly played, "For Now — For Always."

Flat on their stomachs, the twins watched the scene on the terrace below from their hiding place on the balcony. Words — not the words they wanted to hear — reached their ears plainly. Dinner had begun so wonderfully, but now two voices were sharp in anger.

"Well, don't worry!" Margaret McKendrick snapped. "I'm leaving in the morning with Sharon!"

Sadly, the twins watched their mother fling down her napkin, rise, and walk rapidly into the house.

The girls watched as their father sat for a moment with his head in his hands. Then he walked slowly in the direction of the garage. Soon, they saw his convertible roll out on the drive.

"Well! What a mess they made of *that!*" Susan exclaimed.

"And after all we've done to bring them together." Sharon groaned. "I guess we've lost out, Susan. You heard. And Mother and I will be leaving in the morning."

"Don't give up, Sharon. We've got all night to think of something."

"What else can we possibly think of?"

"How do I know?" Susan said crossly. "The important thing is, we've got to think. Come on!"

Vicky Goes Camping

THE BREAKFAST SMELL of coffee, toast, and bacon wafted up the stairs. Maggie stood at the bottom step. "Sharon! I'm waiting!"

"Just a minute, Mother!" Sharon called down.

Mitch walked into the living room. "I'm sorry, Maggie. I — I'll send Susan to Boston at Easter."

Maggie pulled on her gloves. "I'm sorry too, Mitch, but you'll have Sharon for Christmas. We can plan more completely later."

"What d'you mean?"

"Oh, both of them for six months with me — six with you. Susan called it 'the six-month split.' She said that's what the children at camp called it."

"Oh."

"Yes."

"Well, I s'pose it's the best way," Mitch said.

"I suppose so. Sharon! Hurry up!" Margaret looked down at her gloves.

At the thud of footsteps on the staircase, both parents looked up. Sharon and Susan, both in jeans and identical T-shirts, thumped down the stairs.

"What is this, Sharon?" Maggie asked, looking from one girl to the other. "Why aren't you dressed?"

"Well, we've come to a decision, Mother," one of the twins said. "We decided that we've been gypped."

"What do you mean 'gypped'?" asked their father.

"Gypped — cheated out of a campout in the mountains. We've decided to spend it together. Both of us."

"Oh?"

"Sharon," Maggie said, sharply, "put on your suit, this minute!"

"Am I Sharon? Hard to tell, isn't it?" said one twin.

"Am I Sharon? Hard to tell, isn't it?" echoed the other.

"Don't get smart with me, girls!" Maggie exclaimed.

"Well?" they asked together, and looked from their mother to their father.

Their parents looked at them, then at each other. "I don't know! Can you tell?" their father asked. Their mother shook her head.

"Well, then, this is the plan. We leave for the camp-out immediately. When we get back on Friday, we'll tell you who's Sharon and who's Sue."

Maggie and Mitch stared at each other with — was it dismay or relief?

"Well?" asked both twins.

Mitch shrugged. "Well — I guess we don't have a choice — since we can't choose between them."

Out in the driveway the girls helped Hecky stack sleeping bags and other camping gear into the back of the pickup truck. Ahead of them in the driveway stood Vicky's convertible. Behind the wheel sat Vicky talking furiously with Mitch.

From the platform of the pickup, Sue and Sharon watched with keen interest.

"Poor Daddy. I guess he's in trouble." They watched Vicky's hand thump on the steering wheel. "She's making a regular speech," Sharon said.

Their mother walked out of the house, dressed for camping. "Gosh! Here comes Mother in slacks and boots!" Sharon exclaimed.

"Well, what did you expect her to wear on a camping trip?" Sue asked. "She's not exactly going to a tea party!"

"Hello, Vicky!" their mother called. "Beautiful morning!"

"We'd better get over there, Susan. Mother sounds a little too sweet for me," Sharon said.

"Like a welcoming committee!" Susan agreed, jumping to the ground.

"Wait a minute, Susan!" Sharon leaped down. "Do you suppose Mother has some plan of her own?"

Just then they heard their mother say, "No, Mitch! Vicky is perfectly right. I completely agree with her. What will people think? You can't go off and leave behind the girl you expect to marry! No! Now, I insist. I'll stay here and Vicky will go. All right, Vicky?"

"My gosh!" Sue groaned. "If that's a plan, we're sunk!"

"Well, I guess we'd better go over, anyway. Maybe we can do something," Sharon said.

But it was too late. Mother was already leading Vicky into the house, to outfit her with camping clothes!

They rode along the smooth highway for a short while, then turned off to begin the climb along the bumpy mountain road. Susan and Sharon bounced in the back of the pickup. Hecky, his wide-brimmed hat pulled over his face, lay stretched out on the camping gear.

"Sound asleep!" Susan said.

"I don't know how he can sleep bouncing around like this!" Sharon answered.

"Sharon, did you see Vicky's face when Mother said 'Now watch out for snakes'?" Susan giggled.

"Did I! And when Mother said the trip would give her a chance to get acquainted with us, I thought Vicky was going to back out of it."

"I wish she had," Susan said soberly. "In fact, what I noticed most was Mother's saying to Vicky: 'After all, you'll have them for six months each year.' Sharon, we've got to stop this. Can you imagine six months with Vicky?"

"I still think that Mother has some sort of a plan," Sharon answered.

"I just hope she knows what she's doing," Susan said. "If it's a plan, *I* think it's *insane!*"

"Susan!"

"Well, she sure smashed up our plan," Susan said crossly. "Gosh, we could have been camping up in the mountain like a real family — just for a change!"

"What are you kids gabbing about?" Hecky said suddenly, from under his hat. "A man can't get any sleep around here."

"Time you woke up, Hecky," Susan said. "We're close to pile-out."

"What's pile-out?" Sharon asked, puzzled.

"That's the place where Hecky gets the mules. They carry the heavy supplies and we carry our knapsacks — and walk. Up, up, up."

After they had climbed steadily for about fifteen minutes, Mitch flung down his knapsack.

"Why are we stopping here, Daddy?" Susan asked.

"Vicky's not used to this, honey. We'll rest a minute, huh?"

"Oh." Susan looked over to where Vicky was seated on a rock.

"Vicky," Mitch called to her, "I'm walking back to check on the pack mules and Hecky. You rest now. The lake's only about another hour's walking." He started back down along the steep mountain trail.

Vicky looked after him. Her expression was not kindly but she didn't say anything.

Sharon pointed to the foot of a pine tree. "Look, Susan. What is that?"

"Nothing but a little tree lizard," Sue replied.

"Isn't it dangerous?"

"Nope." Susan bent over and swiftly picked it up. "I've got an idea." She placed it gently on the spout of her water canteen and walked over to Vicky.

"Hot, isn't it?" she asked.

Vicky looked at her crossly. "What of it?" She rubbed her booted foot.

"Well, just thought you might like a drink." Susan held out the canteen.

Vicky reached out for it. She lifted it up to her lips. Over the spout, the dragon-like little creature stared solemnly into her eyes. "EEeek!" She screamed and sent the canteen flying. Susan caught it.

Hecky and the pack train came up the trail and into the clearing. Mitch followed behind. "Say, did I hear a scream?" he asked as he walked up. "Why, Vicky! What's wrong?"

"It was just a little ol' tree lizard, Daddy. Look!" Susan held it up.

Her father looked at her steadily. "Cut it out. Understand?" He took Vicky's hand. "It wouldn't hurt you, Vicky."

"Get it away!" she sobbed. "I hate crawly things!"

Mitch turned to the twins. "Now listen, girls. Hecky and I are going on ahead to set up camp. You stay here and help Vicky. Do you understand?"

The girls nodded. He turned to Vicky. "As soon as

you're rested, you three folks follow along. You can't get lost. Straight up the trail." He strode off to catch up with Hecky who was leading the mules up the steep slope.

Vicky glared at the girls. "You'll *help* me, I know — right over a cliff." She rubbed her foot. "But watch out, girls. I can make your lives miserable you know — later. Get it?"

Susan walked away. "Sharon," she called, "you'd better help me."

"Help how?" Sharon called back.

"We've got to get clapping sticks in case of mountain lions."

"Mountain lions!" Vicky gasped. "Wait, Sharon! I'm coming too!"

Soon each of the three had a pair of sticks. Sue led the way, clicking the sticks together first to the right, then to the left, all along the trail.

"There's the lake!" Sharon cried, after they had been walking and clicking for nearly an hour. "Look! Daddy and Hecky have one tent up already!"

"Guess we're safe now," Susan said. "We can stop hitting these sticks."

"Well, thank goodness!" Vicky exclaimed. "I've already got a blister!"

"Hi, girls! See you made it," Mitch called.

"It was easy. Oh boy, look at that lovely lake. Me for swimming, Daddy!" Sue shouted.

"Me too!" Sharon cried.

They ran down to the clearing. Vicky came limping behind them.

"Why don't you get into a suit too, Vicky? You look awfully hot," Mitch said.

"Not me," Vicky said shortly. She looked at her dusty boots. "Maybe I will go wading, though. My feet are killing me."

"Sure! Go ahead. We'll have a tent set up for you in a minute. Boy! Isn't this mountain air something!"

"Are you going to swim?" Vicky asked.

"Who, me? Heck, no! I've gotta fish for our dinner."

"*Fish!* You mean we're going to have *fish?*"

Mitch looked surprised. "Sure we're going to have fish. Why, Vicky, that's what a camping trip is all about! Fish."

"Well, I can't stand them!" Vicky snapped.

Mitch scratched his head. "Well — "

"Vicky!" Susan called out as she and Sharon came down the short slope. "Aren't you coming with us?"

Mitch put his arm around Vicky's shoulder. "No, girls. Vicky's just going to do a little wading. She's just going to soak her feet. It'll do them good."

"O.K. Well, here goes!" Susan ran past them and into the cold lake water. Sharon raced behind her. They plunged all-over wet, then stood up, dripping.

"I don't think Daddy is very romantic," Sharon said. "Do you?"

"Hadn't thought about it. Why?"

"Well, imagine saying Vicky is going to 'soak her feet.' That's a very unromantic statement, in my opinion."

"Do you think it would be more romantic if Daddy had said, 'Vicky is going to soak her head'?" Sue asked, giggling.

"Oh, Susan! Honestly, you're almost just like Daddy!"

"Well, I've just given myself an idea. How are you on holding your breath under water?"

"Why?"

"Well, when Vicky comes down to go wading, we can be about in waist-deep water. Only I'll be standing on you, and it will look as though it's only wading-deep. And I'll yell, 'Come on out, the water's fine' — or something."

Sharon giggled. "Well, sure. I guess I could hold my breath. But she'll have to wade *fast!*"

"Don't worry. This lake bottom doesn't slope. It just gets deep in a hurry."

"Well, let's get organized," Sharon said. "Here she comes now."

It was Hecky who helped Vicky to flounder, screeching pitifully, to her feet. Her blonde hair hung lank and dripping.

"My wiglet!" she screamed. "I've lost my wiglet."

Hecky yelled, "Mitch! Hey, Mitch!"

The twins' father was already running down to the lake edge. "What's happened? What's wrong?"

Hecky led the dripping Vicky to dry ground. "Lost her wiglet," he said shortly.

"Her *wiglet!*" Mitch stared. "What's her wiglet?" He put his arm around the sobbing Vicky.

Hecky shrugged. "I didn't like to ask," he said.

All Is Lost; Or Is It?

THE FIRST STARS were winking in the sky by the time the campers were seated around the fire eating the delicious mountain lake trout Mitch and Hecky had caught.

"Hecky, you really did yourself proud! Got another of these?" Mitch held out his plate. "How about you, Vicky? Ready for another?"

"I detest fish," Vicky snapped. "How many times do I have to tell you? I ate this one only because I was starving. I'll wait and eat in the morning. What are we having for breakfast?"

"Trout," Hecky said.

"Sure, Vicky. We don't catch fish just to throw them

away," Mitch added. "We always eat off the trail out here. That's part of the fun!"

"Only part of the fun? What's the other part? Throwing rocks in the lake?"

"Look, you insisted on coming," Mitch said. "Now the least you can do is to make the best of it."

Susan gently pressed her elbow into Sharon's ribs.

"Insisted! *Insisted!*" Vicky blurted. "I was *tricked* into coming. *She* tricked me!"

The twins' father burst out laughing. "Why, I guess she did at that! Oh well, come on, Vicky. Nothing's that bad!"

Vicky glared.

Mitch stopped laughing. "If you want to go back,

Hecky can always take you back down," he said quietly.

"Sure, miss. I'd be happy to walk you down to the truck," Hecky offered.

"No thanks," Vicky snapped. "I'm going to stick it out." As if to prove her point, she picked up two sticks from the ground beside her, and arose.

Clack, clack — right. Clack, clack — left. She walked toward her tent.

"What's she doing?" Mitch asked, puzzled. Hecky shook his head.

"Hey, Vicky! What are you doing?" Mitch called.

"Well, what do you think I'm doing? I'm keeping mountain lions away — naturally!"

"Mountain lions!"

"The noise." Vicky clacked the sticks. "Doesn't the noise frighten mountain lions away?"

"Not a bit."

Vicky slammed the sticks to the ground. "Good night!" She disappeared into the tent.

The pine knots hissed in the campfire. Hecky gathered up the plates. Mitch looked at the twins. "Now just why did you do that to Vicky?" he asked sternly.

"Us?" Susan asked.

"Yes — 'us.'"

"Why, Daddy!"

"Why, Daddy! Well, I don't want anymore of that from either of you. Understand?"

"Yes, Daddy."

"Yes, Daddy."

Mitch tried to glare at them, but turned away quickly. Susan was pretty sure he was hiding a smile.

Much later that night Sharon lifted the tent flap and looked out. Snores came from her father's and Hecky's sleeping bags on the other side of the clearing. The moon was sailing high and cold above the Douglas firs. Sharon ducked back into the tent. "O.K. Everything's quiet," she whispered to Susan.

"Got the twine?" Susan asked. She unscrewed the lid of a jar of honey.

"You know, I've secretly wanted to clobber a tent ever since Camp Inch's famous Arapahoe clobber," Sharon said.

Susan giggled. "Yes, I guess you could see right away that it gives you a chance to be artistic."

Sharon hesitated. "It is sort of mean. Maybe we shouldn't."

"Well, for the love of Mike. Sure it's mean. Do you want to be *nice?* Don't forget how nice she'd be to us six months out of a year!"

"Well, I guess it's all part of what Mother said — it will give Vicky a chance to get acquainted with us." The girls giggled nervously.

"I'm ready. Are you?" Susan asked.

"Come on!" Sharon led the way.

Scream after scream raked the early morning quiet. "Get them away from here! Help! HELP!"

Susan and Sharon struggled out of their sleeping bags. Susan whispered, "Boy! She's having a fit. Must be ants in the honey!"

Sharon was first at the tent flap. "Ants!" she cried. "It's *bears!* Susan! Look!"

Sure enough! Two black bear cubs came tumbling ahead of Hecky. "Git out o' here. Git!" Hecky scooped a handful of pebbles and flung it after the fat, waddling pair. "Don't be scared, miss," he was saying. "They're only little bitty bear cubs. They wouldn't hurt a fly!"

"I hate this place. I hate this filthy, dirty, awful place!" Vicky sobbed at the top of her lungs.

"Oh boy! Success at last!" Susan giggled. "Come on!"

"Easy, miss," Hecky said.

Vicky, in pajamas and robe, hair in large, pink rollers, lurched out of the tent. She tripped and stumbled in a mesh of twine. "Get me out of this place!" she screamed.

"Now, miss —"

"Shut up! And get me my *boots!*"

Hastily, Hecky dove into the tent.

The twins' father, lather all over his face, came up from the direction of the lake. "What's going on here?" he yelled.

A coffee pot came sailing through the air. He ducked. "I want to go home — *now!*"

Mitch stared at Vicky in amazement. Twine dragged and trailed from her bare feet all the way back into the tent.

"What's happening here?" Mitch asked again. He brushed past Vicky and looked into the tent.

"What's happening? What's happening?" Vicky screamed. "This is what's happening!" She ran straight at Mitch. With every bit of strength she had, she pushed. He stumbled backward, hit the tent pole, and over he went. Down came the canvas on top of him.

"I'm leaving!" Vicky shrieked. "I'm sick of the whole Evers family!" She kicked at the moving heap of canvas.

Hecky shook his head. "Good thing for Mitch she ain't wearin' her boots," he said to the twins.

Vicky, now dressed in camp clothes and boots, came out of the girls' tent. "You can tell your foreman I'm ready to start," she said coldly.

Mitch kept on lathering his face. "Hecky," he called, "she's ready."

Susan held out a head scarf. "Want your clothes, Vicky?"

Vicky snapped it out of her hand. "Thanks. You — you twins. Do you share everything?"

"Everything," Susan said.

"Well, you can give your sister her half of this." She slapped Susan stingingly across the face.

"Hey! Now wait a minute!" Mitch strode up.

"*Wait a minute?* Get out of my way!" She angrily walked past him.

"O.K., miss," Hecky called. "O.K., if you want to start."

Muttering, Vicky stormed off at Hecky's heels.

Susan and Sharon beamed at each other.

"Girls!" their father spoke.

"Yes, Daddy." They walked over to where he stood. He rinsed the lather from his face. "Hand me a towel, Susan."

Susan. The girls looked at each other.

"I'd just like to say something about honey."

"Honey!" both girls exclaimed, in relief.

"Yup, honey. Those little cubs sure loved it, didn't they?"

"They sure did!" Susan laughed.

"Well, that sorta brings me to the point. Where there are cubs, there's usually a mama." He looked from one twin to the other. "She's pretty apt to like honey too."

The girls looked down at their sneakers.

"You mean the mother bear might have followed the honey into Vicky's tent?" Sharon asked, paling a little.

"Yes. And there's no fooling around a she-bear with cubs. She's about the fiercest creature in the woods. Vicky was lucky." Mitch slapped the towel over the tent pole. "As for the rest — well, maybe Vicky and I both learned something. You might start balling that twine, girls. Sure is a mess around here."

Susan stubbed her sneaker into the dirt. "You can't blame Sharon, Daddy. They don't know about bears in Boston. But, gosh! I was just thinking of *ants*. I never thought about *bears*."

"Quite a few things you didn't think of," her father said quietly. "Well, I'm going fishing while things get cleaned up around here. O.K.?"

"O.K."

They watched their father walk off, fishing rod in hand.

Sharon turned to the wrecked tent. "Susan, wasn't that funny? Daddy didn't really say anything about us clobbering Vicky!"

Susan picked up an end of twine. "Well, he's pretty mad though. I can tell."

Sharon tugged at an end of canvas. "Susan — you don't suppose we've driven Daddy right into Vicky's arms?"

"Oh, for gosh sakes! Don't be so dramatic!"

"Well, it sure looks as though we've driven him out of ours!" Sharon said, gloomily.

"Sure does." Susan sighed, and began winding twine.

"For Now—For Always"

Lights burned bright in the kitchen as the pickup came crunching up the dark drive. Mitch drove on past and stopped in front of the garage. The twins climbed out from the back. "I'm frozen," Sharon said. "I can't believe it's still summer."

"You go on up to the house, Sharon. I'm going to help Hecky with the gear," Susan said.

"O.K." Sharon ran to the house.

"Mother! Where are you?" she called as she opened the door.

Her mother stepped from the other side of the open refrigerator door. "Well, hi!" She slammed the door shut with her knee and carried a big salad bowl over to the table. "I didn't hear you drive up. You're just in time for some food." She laughed. "By the way, who are you?"

"Sharon. Gosh, Mother — Daddy's coming in any minute — and you're barefooted!"

Her mother burst out laughing. "Well, what do you think he'll do? Boil me in oil, or send me back to Boston?"

"Well, couldn't you at least put on sandals?" Sharon groaned.

"Oh! I see your point!" Maggie exclaimed. "You mean I look as though I'm camping out?"

"Well, yes."

"Now, dear, I never have the chance to go barefoot in Boston. Live and let live! That's what I'm learning! Tell me — did everybody have a wonderful time?"

"Sensational," Sharon answered. "Well, at least *we* had a wonderful time. I don't think Vicky did."

"What happened?"

Susan and her father came in the back door.

"Hi, Mother." Susan kissed her mother. "How are you?"

"Wonderful. You don't seem so bouncy. What's wrong?"

Mitch strode past. "Well, hi!" Maggie said.

"Good evening." He swung through the door into the dining room.

"Well!" Maggie turned to her daughters. "Have you had your dinners?"

"We're not hungry," Sharon said.

Maggie looked quickly from one to the other. "Maybe you will be after a nice hot bath. You two look pretty grubby to me."

"O.K." The twins, looking droopy as well as grubby, left the kitchen. Sharon turned back. "We'll tell you about Vicky, but not while *he's* here."

"Ssh. O.K.!" Maggie said.

Scrubbed, in clean pajamas and warm robes, Susan and Sharon walked slowly downstairs.

"We'd better get it over with," Susan said. "We sure blew it."

Sharon's chin trembled. "We sure did. Daddy hardly *spoke* to Mother."

"And Mother didn't even seem to mind," Susan added. "I guess it's just about impossible to fix up other people's lives." Sharon sighed.

"Oh, I don't know. I think we've fixed up Daddy's — we've *clobbered* it," Susan replied.

"Well, he clobbered *ours*. And Mother did too! Now we'll just get sent around every six months and everything — and I call that clobbering." Sharon dabbed at her eyes with the back of her wrist.

They reached the bottom of the staircase. Susan put her arm around her sister. "Sharon, don't *bawl*. It isn't dignified."

They walked on to the kitchen.

Their mother was getting more bowls from the refrigerator. Their father leaned against the edge of the sink. He turned. "Well, you kids look considerably improved. Guess I'll go wash my hands."

"Wait, Daddy," Sharon began. "We've been talking."

"Oh?"

"Yes, and we feel that we owe you an apology. Well,

I mean, we feel sort of guilty about what we did to Vicky."

Maggie put down a saucepan. She looked at them in surprise. "What *did* you do to Vicky?"

Mitch looked at her. "You mean to say you don't know?"

"Certainly I don't know. What *did* you do, girls?" Maggie asked sternly.

"Well, I guess you could say we — we submarined her," Sharon replied, looking miserable.

"You sure did," their father said.

"Yes," Susan said. "It's none of our business who you want to marry, Daddy, and we ruined it for you."

Their father thoughtfully rubbed his mouth and chin. He turned to the sink. Water gushed from the tap. "Well, it's done now," he said, his back to them. "We won't talk about it anymore."

"We're really sorry, Daddy," Sharon said. "Will you forgive us?"

"Oh, go to bed, you monkeys," their father replied.

Back in the bedroom Sharon sobbed. "I can be as undignified as I please. Nobody's looking."

"*I'm* looking, for gosh sake. Sharon, will you stop? Listen, you'll be back here for Christmas. That's only — " She held up her fingers. "September, October, Novem — "

"Oh, *stop!*"

"Then you stop."

"O.K." Sharon sat up.

"Listen!" Susan exclaimed. "I hear Daddy's shower running."

"What's so wonderful about that?"

"Well, he *said* he was just going to wash his hands. Sharon, I'll bet he's getting beautified for dinner with Mother!"

"Hmph!" Sharon snorted. "I can't imagine why. She doesn't even have shoes on. He probably got disgusted with all women and left her kerplunk in the kitchen."

Susan went to the window. "Well, the kitchen lights are still going. I can see by the light on the grass."

Minutes passed. Footsteps passed the bedroom door.

"He's going downstairs!" Sharon whispered.

"Let's go out on the balcony!" Susan said.

"Balcony! Why?"

"We can hear better, goop! They might come out on the terrace."

"Well, we'd better take blankets. It's cold out there."

"Oh, Sharon!" Susan groaned. "You probably would really be more comfortable back in Boston."

Sharon's chin began to wiggle again.

"My gosh! Don't do that! Here — let's grab a blanket."

In the cold starlight, the twins huddled close. "I think we might as well go in," Susan said. "They aren't going to come out on the terrace. It *is* too cold."

"I guess *you'd* be 'more comfortable back in Boston!'" Sharon giggled. "Hey! What's that sound?" She leaned forward. "Oh, it's only the hi-fi. I thought — "

"Ssh!"

"What's the — "

"*Ssh!*" Susan held up her hand.

"*For now! For always!*" The words floated up.

"It's their song, Sharon! That's the one Mother was

singing in Boston. You know, the one they played at Martinelli's!"

"Are you sure?"

"Sure!" Susan said excitedly.

Sharon flung back the blanket. "Well, my gosh! Let's go in."

"Go *in!*"

"Certainly," Sharon replied. "We've done all *we* can!" She stood up. "Come on, Susan. It's all up to Mother and Daddy now. Let's just *hope*."

Shivering, they stepped back into the bedroom.

Susan reached out and clicked on the bed lamp. "Sharon! Sharon!" she shook her twin's shoulder.

"Wha's matter?" Sharon rolled over and squinted in the light.

"I just had the craziest dream! Oh my gosh!"

"What?" Sharon propped herself up on one elbow.

"Well, you and I were marching along real slow, sort of funny-like — in organdie dresses. And there was music."

"Go on!"

"Well — the music was coming from someplace, and there were flowers, and people. And Sharon —"

"Yes."

"*Reverend Moseby was there.*"

"Susan! Do you suppose — *Look at my arms!*"

"Look at *mine!*" Sue exclaimed.

"*Goosebumps!*" they exclaimed, together.

It was a beautiful California day. In the distance the Pacific stretched out beneath the soft blue sky. On the

110

sunlit terrace Grandfather and Grandmother McKendrick stood with Susan, Sharon, and Verbena.

"Girls, you look lovely. Pink is your color, by all means!" Grandmother McKendrick beamed approvingly.

"First time I ever saw them in floaty skirts!" Verbena wiped a tear from her eye.

"For goodness' sakes, Verbena! This no time to cry!" Susan exclaimed.

"Not at a *wedding!*" Sharon said.

Hecky stuck his head around the door. "Hey! You bridesmaids ready?"

"Ready!" Susan and Sharon sang out.

"Mercy! We'd better take our seats!" Verbena exclaimed.

. . . there was music . . . and there were flowers . . . and people . . . and Reverend Moseby stood waiting.

Sharon and Susan pressed each other's hands. Their eyes met. The Parent Trap *had* worked!